SAFE TO ASSUME

A Thriller

J. C. FULLER

J.C. Fuller LLC

CONTENTS

INTRODUCTION

Mr. Bertola,

As requested, enclosed are the case notes with my final thoughts included at the end.

Please bear in mind the file was originally split in two: The confession letter and the voice memo recordings. Since the timeline on both prospectives vary, I've taken the liberty of sorting the documents and alternating between the two points of view. This will hopefully correlate the separate incidents, placing them in the order I believe they occurred, and giving you a fuller understanding of the events that followed.

Note: I feel compelled to give you a warning. Though not described in graphic detail, the following topics are referenced throughout this case:

- Missing Person/s
- Stalking: In person/Internet
- Abduction
- Misrepresentation of oneself/Catfishing
- Harassment/Bullying

- Abusive Language
- Marital Infidelity
- Abuse of Drugs
- Murder/Suicide
- Sex without consent
- Death of a Parent/Sibling
- Criminal Acts Minor/Major

1

"Mr. Clean"

Case# 608437
Evidence# 04-291
Typed Confession Letter

The second she saw me I knew she was disappointed.

The nervous recovery of her smile, the slight droop in her shoulders, the hesitant jerk in her step as she crossed the small coffee shop towards me. All visible cues I was not what she had expected, or rather, hoped for.

But that is the chance you take with online dating.

Not that I had set out to deceive her. No, I'd been honest. Confessed upfront I was terrible at selfies. My dating website pictures a few years older, taken before I'd become a gym rat.

I'm pretty sure the body builder description is what landed me the coffee date, and though I tried to be clear that I was only a beginner, it was obvious she had expectations of meeting a guy whose biceps and pecks strained against his polo shirt, barely contained. No wonder she was disappointed.

And then there was my profile name. Mr. Clean.

Aged thirty with a receding hairline, I thought the shaved look suited me best. Oh, and then there was also the lifting competition angle... You gotta shave everything. Chest, legs, arms. Even your ass. The guys at the gym had coined the nickname, which I wasn't a fan of, but they were bigger and stronger than me, and I wanted to fit in, so I didn't argue. It became my persona.

There she was, a smile plastered in place with a falsehood of politeness, greeting me, an anemic Mr. Clean lookalike, minus the all-white attire. She was even prettier in person, so I returned her smile, and stood, hoping my six-foot-three height would redeem my lackluster physique, and pulled out her chair. This garnered a genuine grin as expected. Being a gentleman has always served me well.

We struggled for a bit with conversation and eye contact, her attention swiveling around the crowded coffee shop, bouncing from face to face. I wondered if maybe she'd been savvy enough to have a friend follow her in. Like a backup ditch plan in case, I was creepy or gave off the wrong kind of vibe. When meeting practical strangers, women need to be careful, so I couldn't take offense... too much. Then again, she could have been checking the exits. Trying to decide if she should bolt. Whatever the reason, she suddenly faced forward and became laser focused on me, giving her full attention while peppering me with "get-to-know-you-better" questions. In other words, I was being interviewed.

I did my best to be open. My eyes roaming her face, taking in her natural beauty. The smattering of pink in her complexion, the fullness of her lips, the dimples in her cheeks. Noted the way her fingers folded and unfolded the paper straw wrapper, a sure sign she was a fidgeter or nervous. How, when she took a sip of her coffee, she had a perfect pucker, licking her lips after every sip. I couldn't help but stare.

She reminded me of a beautiful bobblehead, nodding politely at my answers, giving the proper chuckle or sigh of condolence as I shared my life story...which wasn't much. I was new to town, my parents were dead, no siblings, but I had an aunt who I kept in contact with for holidays. I liked my job, was renting a place, looking to buy, and for hobbies? Well, there was the gym and my body building aspirations, and... uh... movies. Which ones? Oh, the popular ones... the same ones as her.

Now, it was her turn. I asked my leading questions. Who was this girl sitting across from me? What was her story?

Full confession? I knew most of it just from scanning through her socials. She posted about everything from her morning coffee to complaints about work, to what lip stain and shoe combo she wore that day, each meal she ate, and what show or book was currently holding her attention. It wasn't hard to "find things" in common.

We'd reached the part of the date, having played the "tell me more about yourself " game for an hour, to where we'd either call it quits, or venture into the realm of... "I'm getting hungry. You wanna get something to eat?"

Where she could either respond with, "Oh, thanks, but I already have plans," OR "Yeah, I could eat."

Up to a few minutes' prior, I'd have thought her answer would have been along the lines of, "Oh, I can't. But this was nice! We'll have to do it again. I'll call you." ...And then I'd never hear from her again. But there had been a not-so-subtle shift in her body language. She'd begun to lean in, and when I managed to say something remotely funny, she'd give my hand a light touch, her fingers lingering a little longer on my skin each time, her smile wider, her laugh louder.

It boosted my confidence, so when she said, "Sure, I could eat. You wanna try the new place on tenth? We can take your car." I did my best not to act surprised and readily agreed, though I'm not a fan of sushi.

We got up from the table, the coffee shop rush done, and I escorted her out to my car, making sure to unlock and hold open the passenger door. Score another point for chivalry.

Ignoring her subtle jab about the late age of my BMW and its pristine cleanliness, I pulled out of the parking lot and onto the road, a headlight out, driving in the direction of 10th street... and then I remembered.

"Would you mind if I stopped by my place real quick? I left my debit card at home, and I don't have enough cash on hand." I'd given my best, harmless grin. Pausing for a split second, she weighed the idea of going to a stranger's house, but since she was already in a stranger's car... in for a penny, in for a pound.

"Sure. Or, I could pay... this time."

"And have you going back to your friends, telling them I pulled the cheapskate, 'I left my wallet at home' bit?" I'd shot her a playful smile to assure I was joking. "It'll only take me a second to run in. Unless you'd like to come inside? Meet my puppy? She's a Frenchie. You like dogs, don't you?" She does, and I already know this.

"I adore Frenchies!" she practically squealed as she clapped her hands, the tires of my car already crunching over the graveled drive.

I threw the beamer into park, and watched, from the corner of my eye, her expression morph from delighted to apprehensive, her neck stretched forward, wide eyes peering up at my house, frowning. She wasn't impressed. I quickly reminded her this was a rental and only temporary. I was looking to buy on the nicer side of town. That seemed to revive her good mood, and she stepped out of the car, letting me take her hand and lead her up the front steps.

A gentleman wouldn't reveal what happened next, but

since all of the world wants to think the worst, I will. She met my dog, and while she sat on my living room floor, playing with Sophie, I offered her something to drink. She accepted, and after a bit, complained she was suddenly tired, not feeling well. I offered to take her home or back to her car at the coffee shop. She declined, and said she'd get an Uber. I took it as the brush off that it was. The interior of my place was even grubbier than the outside.

A few minutes later, there was a ding on her phone, and she said her ride was outside. We exchanged a brief hug, her arms loose, noodle like around my waist, and I walked her to the door. We made a promise to have a follow-up date, and I cracked a joke, promising not to forget my wallet next time, before I opened the door and she departed... safe and sound.

I couldn't tell you what happened to her after she left, other than she disappeared into the ether, only to reappear on newscasts, local and national, as a missing person seventy-two hours later. My days were pure misery because of it for months... until they found her. Buried in a shallow grave.

That's when life became a living hell.

2

Lydia

Case# 608437
Evidence# 05-4333
Recovered Voice Journal-Transcript-Timeline Unknown

I got to thinking... for posterity, it might be wise to document this journey. Easier if I dictate. That way, if I need to omit anything... for legal reasons, I can leave those bits out. Safer that way. Well, then. Let me start with number three... uh, victim number three, that is.

I hadn't recognized the photo, the one they flashed across the screen with bold letters captioned above, LOCAL MISSING WOMAN. No surprise, since the news room used a driver's license photo, which I think we can all agree, is a far cry from a glamour shot.

I'd glanced at the screen as I crossed the living room into

my kitchen, intent on making a fruit smoothie for breakfast, and was only half listening, as I was only half awake.

"Have you seen this woman?" The grind of the blender interrupted every few seconds.

"Family members say she hasn't been seen since..."

"Wearing a black pencil skirt, plaid jacket, and a red blouse..."

"A third-grade teacher employed at Roosevelt Elementary..."

That last snippet had caused me to pause, my finger left to hover over the blend button. Roosevelt Elementary was where my sister had taught. A few hurried steps out of the kitchen, and I was back in my living room, blender pitcher in hand, scrutinizing the screen.

"If you have any information on the whereabouts of Charlene Sutton, please contact..."

"Shit!"

My jaw had hit the floor. I knew the missing woman! Had chatted with her in passing at the grocery store only a few months back. We'd made idle chit chat while waiting our turn in the deli line, sharing a secret smile as a "Karen" made a big stink over the lack of blue in her blue cheese.

Maybe she hadn't recognized me? I'd always liked Charlene... despite everything that had happened.

The station switched to a commercial, so I fumbled for the remote, hoping to catch the competition's newscast. Once again, Charlene's face appeared upon the screen, this time a profile picture from one of her socials, along with an appeal for information regarding her location. I listened with rapt attention as I scribbled on a notepad I didn't remember grabbing. Dates, times, last location... the call for search volunteers.

Volunteers? I could help! Here was a call for aid and I would answer! Atone. Shred this shroud of shame that hung over my spirit. I had more than enough vacation time, thanks to a tropical storm wiping out my holiday destination, a tiny island in the South Pacific. A week ago, I'd been beyond pissed to cancel, but now, it seemed ordained. And I was sure Charlene's parents would be grateful for the help. Regardless from where it came from... right?

It turned out that they were. That the past was the past and all that mattered was locating Charlene. I knew I'd be the one to find her. That this was the way I could make up for the past. I felt it in my gut.

Unfortunately, my gut was wrong. I wasn't the one. A group of hunters on a frosty October dawn stumbled across her in an open field, bloody and bruised... long dead. Naked, dirty, tortured. She'd fought her attacker tooth and nail, but he'd overtaken her, had his way, and then left her to die in the bitter cold... which was probably sweet relief.

It broke my heart I'd not been the one to find Charlene, and I bemoaned being an ostrich in the sand with regards to the two women before her. But the fourth...

Leticia Lopez was her name. I didn't know her, not in the least, not like Charlene. So, you may ask, why did I care? Well, though my intentions were and are pure, I confess, I felt a new self-worth in the searching. I, at least, was a good person. I was part of the solution, a driving force for good. I mattered and was unabashed by my desire and dedication, my calling to search for these poor missing souls.

It was nothing to donate my weekends, sacrifice vacations and personal days. Trudge through backwoods and dark alleys every holiday, steadily ignoring my parent's calls and dinner invitations. I could lie and pretend I'd rather be doing anything else, but really, it was and is a need... a compulsion. It probably stems from my sister's case.

Oh, she never went missing. Nothing like that. She was a victim of a murder suicide. Victim is probably the wrong word, since she's the one, according to the police, who pulled the trigger. Her lover had wanted to go back to his wife and... my sister apparently couldn't live life without him. Leaving Charlene Sutton, no choice, but to do just that. Poor Charlene. She even came to my sister's funeral to show her respects. Hard to know if my family would have done the same, if roles had been reversed.

Anyway, back to the subject at hand... It was a Saturday and I'd gone out to search, on my own, wearing my customary orange fluorescent vest and cap. An attempt to avoid being target practice for a nearsighted or drunk hunter. I also carried a long stick. Practical for more than just walking, I used it for protection, along with sweeping the pine needled forest floors and overgrown pastures.

It was a corn field that morning. The stalks tall and green, the leaves sharp and ridged, silk spiking out of the ears... and in the very middle of the labyrinth of rows was Leticia.

Reality isn't like television. If my experience had been like an episode of Dateline, help and resources would have arrived a short time after my call into 9-1-1. To the viewer, it seems instantaneous. In the real world, I was left with a bloated and battered body for over an hour.

In a situation like that, where you have ample time to examin the handiwork of a sadistic madman, you find yourself making promises to the dead. Apologizing for sins that are not your own, and in my case, swearing oaths of binding. Promises of the heart.

My promise? I'd find who did this to her...or die trying.

"Mr. Clean"

Case# 608437
Evidence# 04-291
Typed confession letter– Undated

It's difficult to dispose of a body without leaving a trace of evidential DNA. I mean, a partial thumb print, a wayward eyelash or plucked arm hair could give the game away. Short of wearing a full body suit...or shaving yourself from head to toe, it is damn near impossible. Or so I would assume. Just like you.

Not to mention, dumping the remains without leaving some type of footprint. Not a literal shoe impression, though that would be a real concern. I'm talking digital. Everything from cell phone towers and vehicle GPS systems, to cameras lining freeways and the front porch of every neighbor in a five-mile radius. The skill or amount of luck you'd have to have to make a whole person disappear without a trace... those are Vegas odds and I'm not that lucky.

Suspicion fell on me right away, though in all fairness, I'd not been very clever. Petrified, would be a better description.

I had chosen, despite recognizing the name and picture on the screen, to not call the information hotline and report my encounter with the missing woman. It was stupid and cowardly, and in retrospect, I'm not proud I turned a deaf ear to her family's plea for any news or insight to her whereabouts.

I had hoped it would all just go away. That she'd be found, hopefully safe, in some hospital room after a fender bender, or maybe... off on a last-minute business trip, stuck on some airplane, forty thousand feet up in the air, unable to call. I mean, after all, what could any of it have to do with me? A lot can happen to someone in four days.

My second mistake was deleting my dating profile.

When the cops showed up at my door, it was an utter surprise. They'd located her vehicle still parked at the coffee shop, and after burning some shoe leather, were able to get my description and license plate number from a very observant barista... Glad I didn't tip.

I wanted to appear helpful. Why wouldn't I be? Told the detectives about our "date" and how the evening came to an abrupt end. She'd left my house around seven, in what I assumed was an Uber, and I'd not heard from her since. Did I find it odd to not have gotten a text later that night or maybe, the next day? No, not at all. She'd clearly given me the brush off. Was I resentful? Well, it didn't make me feel good.

I suppose, lawyering up right away was also another mistake. But what choice did I really have? I didn't care for the way the detectives were eyeing me or the questions they were asking. They appeared excitedly anxious and overly desperate.

Time was not on their side, and the fact that this was the seventh woman to be snatched off the streets... they were eager for a solution. To find someone they could point out and offer up to the lynching mob, granting them a moments reprieve from their superiors at city hall.

And well, I fit the profile. Single male, new to the area, loner down on his luck, above average intellect, with a hobby bordering on obsession. At least, I suppose that's how they saw me.

When I refused to allow them to "look around", expressing, "I'd prefer to have my lawyer present." That's the moment their tunnel vision began.

I can't prove it, but my expensive lawyer agrees, they retaliated by leaking my name to the media. Within hours, a litany of news vans and reporters were stationed outside of my house, shouting questions at my closed doors and windows, calling my cell phone from "unavailable" or "blocked" numbers.

My picture and name were on the evening news, and within a matter of days, the verbiage had changed from "person of interest" to "suspected killer." High class reporting at its best.

My gym nickname of Mr. Clean played well with the media....in that, it made perfect click bait, alongside exterior photos of my rental house, which was in dire need of a paint job.

The inside wasn't much better after the search warrant was executed. They'd torn into the floorboards, pulled up carpet, smashed holes in the drywall, and took the drains from my tub and sinks. Bagged half of my medicine cabinet and confiscated all of my supplements and protein powders, anything that could have been administered to an unsuspecting victim. Didn't stop there either. Towed my car and hauled off my weights, dumb bells, and press bench, even my rubber resistant bands. Oh, and a tool box with everything in it...hammers, set of screw drivers, a crow bar... pliers. Things they construed to be potential weapons of destruction. They cleaned me out.

Any sympathy I had for my neighbors, their lawns and flowerbeds trampled by lookie loos and nosey parkers, quickly vanished. I recognized the old hag across the street and the preppy-ass with the big house on the corner, their faces popping up on my television screen describing how I kept "odd hours," as if being an early riser and a night owl was a crime, and complaining how I seemed "unfriendly" and get this, "too quiet."

Every finger seemed to be pointing in my direction, and despite the prediction I wouldn't be getting my cleaning deposit back after the state the cops left my house, there was the issue of Sophie, my French bulldog. She wasn't actually mine.

I'd found her on one of my morning jogs, collared, but no tag. Shivering and whining, hidden in a bush. I had snatched her up with the full intention of dropping her off at the no-kill shelter on my way into work. But... I was lonely and Sophie filled a void.

That was the final nail in my coffin.

You see, Detective Miller thought he recognized the pooch, and with search warrant in hand and a hunch, he took Sophie down to the vet. Confirmed she was chipped. I felt guilty about that. Frenchies are expensive, and despite finding her out in the cold in the middle of October, I could tell she'd been well taken care of. I shouldn't have been so selfish as to keep her, and it would have been one less point against me, because Sophie belonged to a woman named Leticia Lopez, who'd gone missing over six months ago. Well, was missing. She'd been found.

LOST DOG

Friendly, female Grey French Bulldog

Answers to Lulu. Call ▮▮▮▮▮▮▮▮

REWARD if found and returned.

4

Lydia

Case# 608437
Evidence# 05-4333
Recovered voice journal-Transcript

How did I plan on fulfilling my promise?

The first step was to create a command center. I decided to clear out my spare bedroom, and lug that heavier-than-shit-hand-me-down old mattress to the street corner. Pinned a "Free" sign, smack in the middle. It was gone before noon.

I then went on an office supply shopping spree, where I bought the largest corkboard I could find, along with an equally, impressive in size, eraser board. Both were a bitch to fit in my Subaru, and I'd spent a crap ton more than I'd expected. Those four-in-one printers are cheap. The ink is not.

Next, I jotted over to the local fabric store for some sewing pins and red yarn. So, I could, you know, connect the dots... like they do in the movies.

It took me all day, but I got everything set up. Even managed to drag the cheap desk I scored at Goodwill up the stairs without slipping a disk. Yay, me.

Hooking up my old gaming computer to the new printer, that was the biggest pain. Weak wi-fi signal is such a nightmare, but if the coffee shop down the street is willing to offer it for free... Listen, I know I just boasted about a shopping spree, but the truth is, money is tight, and the room on my credit card is limited.

Thank goodness libraries are free! A great source for information and completely underutilized, it's where I got my research material. That, and streaming free episodes of Dateline, CSI, and Criminal Minds. I tried to consume anything and everything serial killer related, before moving on to FBI profiling and police procedurals: evidence collection, fingerprint analysis, DNA testing, genetics, autopsy reports, witness statements... You get the idea.

After a few months, I felt I was as knowledgeable, even more so, than the clueless saps investigating. They'd yet to find the killer or even a viable suspect, and without a single fingerprint lifted, shoe impression casted, or DNA sample sent in for testing, they were obviously biding their time. Sadistically hoping for another victim, and praying the killer would make a mistake! Offering up a sacrificial lamb, as far as I was concerned.

In addition to my education efforts, my late night reading consisted of every scrap of public information I could obtain regarding the prior deaths. I hadn't gotten involved until Charlene Sutton, and I knew plenty about Leticia Lopez. Very little about the two women that came before them.

They were around the same age as the others, single or

freshly unattached. Attractive, athletic, social, pet owners. It was easy to spot the similarities. Their differences were just as obvious. Hair color, eye color, ethnicity... all different.

It got me to wondering... what did these women, on a deeper level, have in common? My mind had swirled with the possibilities and I admit, I started too close. Too personal. I needed more information than old newspaper clippings could provide, and knowing firsthand the desperation and desire for things to be resolved, as in my sister's case, I took it upon myself to try and interview the victim's families. Ask the very personal questions I wanted answers to. Like, what kind of perfume did they wear? Granny panties or G-string? Boob job or mother nature? Pajamas or au naturel? Brazilian or bush? You see where I am going with this? Things that might entice an unhinged pervert to give them notice.

Leticia's family was more than willing to speak with me. Which was no surprise, since I'd been the one to find her. I'm sure they felt grateful, if not a little obligated to be of assistance. The other families were more guarded, tight lipped, wary of this stranger calling them out of the blue. I was forced to lie in an effort to garner their participation and trust, because, well... simply being a concerned citizen...that wouldn't get me past their manicured lawn, let alone, through the front door. I'm not proud of it, but it was for their own good. I claimed to be a producer for Dateline. That loosened their tongues.

I collected and logged every detail given, tracking it all on an Excel sheet. If I was successful in my hunt, this data would ultimately be handed over to law enforcement and used as evidence for the prosecution. It made me giddy to think that one day it might be presented in court!

When I couldn't find a connection in the intimate details of their lives, I broadened the scope.

Did they share a profession or educational background?

How close did they live to one another? Did they belong to the same gym? Drive the same kind of car? Go to the same salon? Share the same veterinarian? Maybe, they shopped at the same grocery store?

Ahhh... That was the question which led to my first legit lead. Something tangible. Something the police hadn't connected, and oh, how complimentary and gracious they had been when I'd showed up at the station with evidence in hand. More like embarrassed.

The first woman to have gone missing, Jillian Mason, worked as a pharmacist's assistant at the local grocery store. She disappeared somewhere between the front doors and her vehicle, which had been parked in the back, beside a large grouping of shrubbery, under a broken street light. Grainy video footage, barely discernible, had caught movement. A dark shadow, someone dressed in all black with considerable height. Not much to go on.

The alarm wasn't raised until the next morning when Jillian's car hadn't moved an inch from its parking spot, and she'd failed to show for her scheduled shift. It dawned on me. If whoever took her didn't use her vehicle to leave the scene, they'd had to have had their own... right? I needed access to the parking lot footage, plus transit videos and street cams. Which entailed spewing more fibs, cashing in a few favors, and promising even more to manage it. It was worth the cost.

I discovered, within a thirty-minute window of her leaving the building, only ten vehicles had pulled out of the neighboring parking lot, a fitness center. The models and license plates, distinctive features such as dents, scrapes, headlights, and broken windshields were all noted.

I moved on to the next victim's presumed snatch site. Addison Morang had gone for an early morning jog, her route looping through the well-lit neighborhood streets before veering off into the wooden trail behind her house.

And then the next, Charlene. She'd been working late. Teacher Parent conferences. Like Jillian, her vehicle had been left behind. Leticia Lopez was the odd ball. She didn't own a car, and either walked or traveled by bus, meaning she had a set schedule. This ended up being a saving grace to my investigation. I didn't like to think how it was also probably what made her such easy pickings.

I spent hours poring over video until I thought I'd go crossed-eyed, But I was committed, and it paid off. I spotted the connection and managed to find what all four girls had in common, succeeding where the police had failed.

A BMW. An older model with circular headlights. One that had followed, or been in the vicinity of each abduction. The color, hard to make out, the videos taken at night, the license plate, nothing but a blur. There was one thing, though. Something that set it apart from all the other vehicles roaming the streets.

The right headlight was out.

5

"Mr. Clean"

Case# 608437
Evidence# 04-291
Typed confession letter

The revelation that Sophie was not my dog resulted in an invitation to the police station for questioning. And by invitation, that meant handcuffed and roughly thrown into the back of an unmarked sedan, reporters and cameras pressed against the window shouting questions and pleas for information.

Their hope, I imagine, was by the time they'd delivered me "downtown," read me my rights, and photographed my arms, hands, and torso, in addition to the media pressure weighing heavy on my shoulders and mind, I'd be rattled and ready to confess.

Except, it had the opposite effect. Come on...I'd suffered at the hands of scarier school yard bullies than these guys. No, I was thick skinned with an expensive lawyer on retainer, and I had rights! They had nothing...not really. I felt defiant!

Oh, but it was still early days. I shouldn't have been so confident.

The interview room they threw me in was small, cramped by an oversized desk, sandwiched between two sets of flimsy, metal chairs. And it smelled like stale beer and vomit. The room temperature didn't help, the heat stuck on high. I was clearly being punished for refusing to speak until my attorney arrived.

They asked questions anyway, and it didn't take long to establish who was playing the "good" cop in the tag team questioning. Detective Miller, wearing a murderous scowl from the second he'd shown up at my door was obviously playing the "bad" cop, leaving Detective Pickard to kindly offer me a glass of water. When I declined, he mentioned it would be no trouble to grab something from the vending machines, if I preferred hot coffee or soda instead. Sneaky bastard. By the way, this gracious offer had come a few minutes after I'd declined to volunteer a DNA sample, flat out refusing to do a mouth swab.

Detective Miller, red faced, fists clenched as tight as his jawline, grounded out that I wasn't doing myself any favors. It looked bad for me, especially with my past record. Had I spoken to my parole officer recently? My return glare, hopefully, clearly stated it was none of his beeswax.

This garnered a sad head shake from good guy Pickard. He, in a fatherly manner, pointed out being unhelpful towards the authorities, making them jump through hoops by getting a search warrant, which the judge would be more than happy to grant, gave the impression I had something to hide. Why waste my time and theirs, and not just volunteer the DNA? An innocent man would...wouldn't he?

It was a good question. One I didn't readily have an answer for, which resulted in an awkward pause...eventually filled by my lawyer, who waltzed into the room with a million dollar smile and scoffed, "Unlikely a judge will sign off on a warrant, when you have no DNA samples to compare it to." My lawyer? Worth. Every. Penny.

They followed this up with an inventory list of questionable items found at my residence. What did a guy like me need with two large rolls of clear plastic found in the basement? My answer, if I'd been allowed to comment, would have been... absolutely nothing. They weren't mine. If the detectives had done some actual detecting, they would have discovered my landlord was a house painter...who apparently, after painting other people's houses, had no energy or desire to paint his rental home. He had a ton of stuff stored in the basement.

From their point of view? The caustic chemicals and bags of cement, the large empty plastic tubs, and empty freezer... Oh, and the aforementioned plastic rolls were a killer's supply list for body disposal. Except, my lawyer pointed out, unless they had receipts or store video showing me purchasing the items in question, they couldn't prove they were actually mine. I saw where he was going with this defense, but to them, it was a moot point. I still had access to everything.

Next, they laid out eight photos, large glossies of the victims, who no longer resembled the pretty faces plastered across television or printed on their missing posters. Detective Miller claimed he and his partner could establish my connection to each one of the women. This was disconcerting at first, but then I reminded myself, the boys in blue are allowed to lie. It could all be a bluff.

Thing was... I knew it wasn't.

Jillian Mason worked at my pharmacy... wasn't super helpful when I forgot my discount card. Allison Morang belonged to my gym...and never wiped down the equipment after use. Charlene Sutton and I had gotten into a fender bender... she'd been at fault, and Leticia Lopez? Well, she worked at my favorite "cheat day" restaurant...always managed to get my to-go order wrong. Oh, then Corin Peterson took her dog to the same Vet as me...her scraggly Chihuahua once picked a fight with Sophie. While Audrey Rae Collins and I shared a dentist...which was ironic, because she never returned a smile. And the last woman, aka, "coffee shop girl"... well, they'd heard it straight from my own mouth. We'd met on an online dating website, and she'd given me the brush off.

On the advice of counsel, I kept my mouth shut. Neither denied or confirmed any association with the victims, and instead, sat back and let my spendy lawyer do the talking. At one point, he had to leave to take a phone call, and "good" cop Detective Pickard confessed in a conspiratory whisper to having a sweet tooth. Even pulled from his pocket a handful of little Dum-Dums lollipops and offered me one. I told him I didn't eat sweets. Boy...his opinion of my intellect was pretty low.

The whole affair took a little over six hours, ending with an idle threat to keep me overnight. Needless to say, I walked out a free man with no charges pressed, only the sensation of holes being burned into my back by the death stares that followed me out.

I thought it was all behind me. They'd not found anything, and likely, wouldn't. Sure, the media was all hot and bothered right now, but my lawyer assured me, they'd be onto something else soon. Hell, election season was just around the corner. The best thing for me to do was lay low. Stay out of the limelight. After all, I hadn't formed any roots in this small town.

"Possibly...," he suggested. "It might be a good time to move on."

I took the hint.

> See attached documentation:
> Evidence# 04-291
> Case-Filed Notes Victim List
> Case# 608437

Appt w/ Mr. Collins
2:30 PM

<u>Track Down</u>
<u>UBER Driver !!</u>

VICTIM LIST

Last Seen ??

Victim # 1   —   Pharmacist Assistant   — Work Parking Lot

Victim # 2 —   Receptionist   — Jogging Trail

Victim # 3 —   Teacher   — School, after hours

Victim # 4 —   Restaurant Mgr.   — Bus Line ??

Victim # 5 —   _______   —

Victim # 6 —   _______   —

Victim # 7 —   _______   — Coffee shop - girl

Gerri —
Old Notes from
my case file.

Victim Timeline # 4 – # 7

Jan Feb Mar Apr May June Jul Aug Sep Oct Nov Dec
                became Lead Det.   # 4 Found   # 5 Missing

Jan Feb Mar Apr May June Jul Aug Sep Oct Nov Dec
    # 5 Found   # 6 Missing   # 6 Found

Jan Feb Mar Apr May June Jul Aug Sep Oct Nov Dec
    # 7 Missing

Lydia

Case# 608437
Evidence# 05-4333
Recovered voice journal- Transcript- Timeline unknown

They failed to warn the public about the BMW with the broken headlight, and by this gross incompetence, made every woman in my town a sitting duck.

When I'd left the police station I expected, within hours, a televised news conference or at the very least, an issued public statement requesting everyone to be on the lookout for the vehicle in question. There was neither. Men's egos are so fragile.

I would have gone to the press myself if Detective Miller, the lead on the case, hadn't suggested my self-involvement was teetering dangerously close to obstruction of justice.

Ticking off his fingers as he listed my apparent misconduct: Interfering with an ongoing investigation, questioning potential witnesses without authorization, tampering with evidence, collecting personal information without consent and by ill-moral means. Seems my impersonation of a Dateline producer had reached their ears.

Without meaning to, I had put myself on the wrong side of the law, becoming a liability instead of an asset. It would be hard to recover from this poor first impression. If I were to approach them again, I'd have to make sure I had solid evidence. Something substantial and concrete. Ideally, irrefutable proof to rub in their noses.

If they wouldn't look for the owner of the BMW, then I would and since I didn't have the DMV database at my fingertips, I called a local used car dealership. Spoke to a very motivated salesperson, who seemed receptive to my request. I was in the market for an older beamer, and if they didn't have any on the lot, I'd pay him to track down private owners in the area, so I could approach them directly... offering cash under the table for his efforts. It was easier than I thought and with my eager bloodhound on the hunt, I turned my attention to my new happy place. Online crime forums.

My favorite being Fans of Dateline, I'd found a plethora of others out there, and each with their own theme, be it kidnappings, missing persons, or serial killers.

Discussing active and cold cases with fellow armchair detectives, while swapping theories and dissecting clues and alibis, thrilled me to my core. I mean, it felt good to be included. Welcomed. I made friends too! It took a bit... you sort of need to prove yourself because not everyone in these forums is an average Joe.

You are conversing with professors, retired and active law enforcement, attorneys and law students, medical doctors, and genetic experts. A melting pot, if you will, of intelligence, sprinkled with regular people, like myself.

Except, I wasn't really what you'd call a regular person, that is, inexperienced. I mean, I did find a dead body. So, as far as the forum members were concerned, I was a superstar... Dare I say, to the newbies of crime fascination, an expert. A select few had even taken my opinions and theories as gospel and were quick to default to my guidance in all thing's true crime. Truly, they think I'm next-level shit! It's like having my own fan club. Or, as I decided to call them, a task force.

There, at my fingertips for the plucking, were potential assets to the investigation. People with surpassing knowledge and experiences beyond my own, who could bring something to the table besides far-fetched speculations and off-the-wall theories, which seemed to poison the less professional forums. Those people were nothing but rookies. Spectators. I wanted hunters. People willing to get their hands dirty... and I found just that.

I created a private chat room and began their education on our quarry. For the exception of Olive, who lives in a neighboring county, no one else had heard of the Manicurist Killer. I know. Such a lame name, and misleading too. It's not like this guy was singling out nail technicians, or women with fake nails as would-be-victims. No. It's because he pulls out their fingernails.

To say this wacko is paranoid about leaving behind DNA is an understatement.

According to the media and the little I was able to glean from the report sprawled across Detective Miller's desk, ... he'd left the office to refill his coffee and I'd taken a little peek. The killer was being described as obsessive and meticulous, leaving nothing to chance.

To me, it was clear with each abduction, this guy had done his homework. Stalked his victims, possibly engaging with them socially before snatching each from a relatively public space. Pretty brazen, considering help was literally around the corner if they were to yell or scream bloody murder. Which meant, either they felt safe in his company, or he'd been able to subdue them in a quick and quiet manner.

I know what you're thinking, I thought the same too, but according to the toxicology report I scanned... By the way, did you know 15% of the population can read upside down? Me neither! I thought everybody could do it, but apparently, it is only a select few. Dumb dumb Detective Miller thought no one could, which is the only excuse I can give him for leaving high class information out in the open for anybody, such as myself, to discover and skim through. Bonehead.

Anyway, the toxicology report showed a narcotic, benzo-diazepine, was used in the latest abductions, detected in the hair samples of the victims. It was unclear if this drug was given seconds after the attack or administered beforehand. Scary as hell either way.

Oh, and did you notice I said the drugs were used in the "latest" abductions? Yeah, the psycho seems to be changing his MO. That is, according to the profile analysis, which I would have given my left arm to read in its entirety. It was poking out from underneath the toxicology report. For a split second, I thought about stuffing it into my purse and strolling out of Detective Miller's office, all nonchalant. The only thing that stopped me, if I'm being honest, was the fear of being caught. His office might have been a cluttered, chaotic nightmare, but he wasn't so dense as to not notice an important FBI report missing. I'm sure he would've put two and two together, and I'd have been toast. So, I refrained.

As I was saying, the killer has been changing things up. However, there has been two things that has remained consistent. One, though always found naked, the victims were never sexually assaulted and two, the pulling of their fingernails. If it hadn't been for the nail removal, I don't know if they'd have tied Charlene Sutton's murder to him, since she was found in an irrigation culvert. The others, they'd been left out in the open, exposed to the elements.

I mentioned before, that this wacko cleans his victims, but when disposing of their bodies, he has no problem rolling them down a ravine, dumping them into the land fill, or tossing them into a deserted corn field to rot. The cleanliness only seems to stem from the desire to destroy DNA, and the fact that his victims are a dirty hot mess when found is no concern to him.

That was until last week, when they found the fifth victim, left inside a huge dumpster outside a rental storage unit.

Corin Peterson. Wrapped head to toe in plastic.

See attached documentation:
Evidence# 05-4334
Handwritten Note
References in Audio Transcript- RECREATED
Case# 608437

TASK FORCE MEMBERS

SCREEN NAME: dTECHtive (Andy)
PURPOSE: IT Guru Experience: Owner of a computer shop in Ohio. (Has connections on the dark web - could be useful.)

SCREEN NAME: DoubleDHelix (Debbie)
PURPOSE: DNA Expert Experience: Studied genetics at Cambridge, Massachusetts before becoming a stay-at-home mom. (Has friends at various labs throughout the U.S.)
— Knows her stuff, very by the book

SCREEN NAME: Private-i (Tom)
PURPOSE: Law Enforcement Expert Experience: Retired NYPD officer (Gun shot wound) Part-time private detective / security guard. — A bit of a know it all.

SCREEN NAME: Alibi Breaker (Olive)
PURPOSE: Inside Scope Experience: Lives four hours away but her brother is a beat cop in town. (small world)
— Works as a secretary at an elementary school. Watches and listens to tons of crime shows / podcasts

SCREEN NAME: GetHLife (Charles)
PURPOSE: Law Expert Experience: Criminal Defense (wants to specialize in small time crime.) — Trying to pass the Georgia bar exam — Thirds times is a charm — Third time is a charm!

"Mr. Clean"

Case# 608437
Evidence# 04-291
Typed confession letter

As predicted, I didn't get my cleaning deposit back.

It took a bit to find a new place, what with all the media attention and the cost of rent these days. Not to mention, who wants to lease their property to a suspected serial killer? I suppose to the cops, it looked as if I was on the run, but really, I had no choice but to cross the state line.

Found an unsuspecting old lady, with no clue who I was, looking to rent out a furnished above garage apartment, her house in the middle of no-where-ville. With first and last month's rent, plus cleaning deposit paid up front, she welcomed me into her home with open arms. Sweet old bitty.

My old landlord didn't give me much time to get my stuff out. Served me with a two-week notice, instead of thirty days. I didn't fight it. I wanted gone as badly as he wanted me out. I gathered my meager belongings into my BMW, and off I went. In truth, I'd hadn't much to pack, the majority of my stuff already sitting in the storage unit.

Yes. I have a rented storage unit. Did the cops ask me about it? No. Should I have informed them? My well-dressed and eloquent lawyer told me, "For Fuck's sake, no!" After all, the warrant applied for, issued, and executed, was only to search my home and vehicle. I was under no obligation to do the cop's job for them. If they weren't smart enough to locate the storage unit, which was paid a year in advance, in cash, then they weren't worth their badge. I happened to agree.

And for more than one reason. I already knew I looked guilty as hell in their eyes, and there were a few stored items, which I felt, would not sway their opinion otherwise. Sure, I had normal junk stored there. Childhood memories, old furniture, boxes of clothing, camping gear, a cheap weight set... my trophies.

I debated on emptying out the unit, scrubbing it clean, moving everything to my new residence, but my lawyer advised against it, sighing, "Better leave it alone. You don't want to draw attention. If the cops have two brains cells, we should assume you're already under surveillance." I'd paid him way too much to argue.

I did as advised and abandoned my storage unit with six months left paid, hoping that when the time for renewal came, the cops would have moved on. The coast would be clear and I'd be able to gather my belongings and move them to a safer location. Regardless, I didn't like the idea of leaving my things behind to be discovered. In retrospect, it was rather stupid of me to have kept anything at all.

At least I had gotten my car back, though, it had been a practical act of congress to retrieve it from the forensic tow yard. Sure, they'd found my date's DNA on the passenger's side of the vehicle, a hair strand attached to the headrest, but as my lawyer argued to the judge, that was to be expected.

She had sat in that very seat on the way to my house. I never claimed she wasn't in my car, and since they'd failed to find her DNA anywhere else in the vehicle, such as the trunk or backseat, there was no reason for them to withhold my only mode of transportation. They also came up with zilch, as I knew they would, when looking for DNA evidence regarding the other women. No blood, stray hairs, broken nails, or fingerprints. Not even carpet fibers. Not a damn thing.

There was nothing they could pin on me. That was, until they'd looked in the glove box and found...a receipt. Crumpled up, stuck way in the back, sandwiched between the pages of an old road map. It was to the landfill.

Circumstantial, not enough to hold my car indefinitely, but one more thing to add to the "guilt" pile of evidence they were compiling. Good thing I shredded everything else.

What I should have done was drill a hole in my computer's hard drive, but like I mentioned earlier, the cops showing up at my door had been a complete surprise. Naive of me, I know.

Call it habit or a guilty conscious, I'd made sure to purge my house after my failed coffee date. If I hadn't, I'm convinced, I'd be sitting in a jail cell right now, destined to be wrongly convicted. With evidence like that, no matter how loquacious my lawyer is, I doubt he would have talked a judge into granting bail.

No, I didn't need to stress about that. I'd covered my tracks. What worried me now were the emails and chat room conversations filled with pointed accusations and veiled threats. Gathered proof of numerous fake social accounts, nothing short of internet stalking. I'd been stupid enough to save it all. I guess I had this misguided notion I'd need it for court someday... when things had finally gone too far. When I couldn't take it anymore.

It would only be a matter of time before the cops decided

to do a deep dive into my computer and social accounts. Have their IT geeks crack and decipher the encrypted files. Ultimately, reaching out to those who I had conversed with, asking them questions, their opinions of me. Discover the obsession, the unrelenting, day in and day out flood of communication. Not to mention all the photos...

Then again, the detectives had bungled so much of the case already, maybe my worries are unfounded. For all I know, my computer is sitting in an evidence cage, collecting dust. No one even giving it a second thought! No one, but me.

It's hard not to. Sitting in this cramped apartment, jobless, friendless, with no internet reception, held to a self-declared conviction of turning over a new leaf. It's nearly impossible not to think about the way I've been treated and how, unfortunately, it will now be perceived.

If you're confused. I wasn't the stalker. I'm the one being stalked.

> See attached documentation:
> Evidence# 04-292
> Landfill Receipt, Copy
> Recovered from suspect's glove box
> Case# 608437

EVIDENCE# 04-292

Landfill Receipt

Copy of Landfill Receipt found in suspect's glove box
Case# 608437

Date: 03/5   Springfield County Landfill
Receipt# 015620

Weighed at Springfield Landfill

Deputy: Ben Evans
Bill to: Cash Customer
Vehicle ID: BMW, LIC. WGTLFTR

Origin: Springfield, City of
TIME IN: 1:30 PM
TIME OUT: 1:57 PM

INBOUND TICKET NUMBER: 01-0063921
SCALE 1 GROSS WT.   2,735 LBS.
SCALE 2 TARE WT.   2,605 LBS.
NET WEIGHT   130 LBS.

QTY   DESCRIPTION   AMOUNT
1   REFUSE $12.00

NET CASH AMOUNT $12.00
AMT. TENDERED $15.00
CHANGE $3.00

Lydia

Case# 608437
Evidence# 05-4333
Recovered Voice Journal-Transcript- Timeline Unknown

Encased in clear plastic. Not a blue tarp or black garbage bag... but transparent. On display.

I think, because I've read one or two books on profiling serial killers, the addition of a covering suggests a barrier. A mental shelter if you will, to separate the killer from his deeds. It allows him to distance his acts, to view his handiwork as if peering through a window pane, an innocent and casual observer. Is he possibly beginning to struggle with guilt? Has remorse for his actions begun to surface? Was there or is there, some emotional connect to Corin Peterson?

Tom... He's retired NYPD, said that was a bunch of bullshit and I should stop romanticizing. The only purpose of the cover, clear or not, was simply to contain the mess and prevent the cross contamination of DNA passing from perp to victim. He ventured, that to the killer, there was nothing special about Corin Peterson, other than the manner she died... Not only had the body been cleansed and fingernails removed, per the typical custom, but the psycho had extracted the teeth as well. It was unclear if this was done before or after severing the head from the body, but either way, this death was much more gruesome than the others. Which, in Tom's opinion, explained the need for extra protection. There was no "meaning" behind the plastic cover. It was simply a new requirement, the clear material being all he had on hand. I guess, we'll agree to disagree.

The added step of removing the teeth interested Debbie, our DNA expert, to no end. Her conclusion? He wasn't escalating in his methods, but rather, it was done in self-preservation. Had Corin managed to bite her attacker? Would they be able, if he were found soon, to compare her bite mark to a bruise on his hand, or forearm? Who knew? I didn't. Which is why having a cohesive team is important for discussions such as this.

Charles, the law guy, suggested it wouldn't matter if he'd been bitten or not. Bite Mark Analysis, though still admissible, was considered unscientific and ridiculously unreliable. Though compelling to a jury, presenting bite mark evidence was thought to be cavalier and sloppy, the history well known. Innocent people having been erroneously convicted due to faulty analysis. Any defense attorney worth his salt, could easily discredit such a comparison if one was provided. He suggested we focus our efforts on finding where the plastic cover was purchased. Receipts and in-store video would be much more damning.

Debbie, who I think was missing the point, argued there

had to be a reason for the change in M.O. In which, Andy, not great with people, but fantastic with computers, said he knew the reason. The guy was a fuckin' psycho. Well... duh.

Olive brought us a bit of exciting news. We now have a fox in the henhouse. Her brother, twisting his ankle while chasing down a purse snatcher, has been put on light duty inside the police station. He's agreed to be our eyes and ears, and keep us abreast of any new developments. Right now, all we get is whatever the authorities leak to the news, which everyone knows, may or may not be the truth, and certainly isn't the whole story.

You may be wondering why her brother is willing to betray his fellow badged brothers. I did too. According to Olive, he has it out for Detective Miller. She wouldn't give us details but said it stemmed back to their days at the police academy. Whatever his reasoning, he has no desire to let the "Manicurist Killer" off the hook, but damn well doesn't want Miller to get the credit for the arrest either. Olive says if he can slip her pertinent information, allowing us to accomplish what Detective Miller has failed to do so far, it would be good enough for him.

To be honest, I doubt he'll be able to gather much intel. He's been assigned to the filing room. But he's better than nothing, and I appreciate his help, regardless of his motivation.

Oh! And speaking of motivation, my used car salesman came through! It's amazing what money can inspire people to do... Though, he was beyond pissed when I handed him only fifty bucks. He rudely reminded me, eyes bulging and neck veins purpling, that I'd promised him five hundred. I bold-faced lied. Told him he must have misheard, and stubbornly held out the fifty until he finally snatched it from my hand. Ungrateful jerk. Fifty bucks was probably more than he'd conjure up within the day working that car lot... The place was a ghost town. He should motivate himself to find a new job!

Anyway, it's a fairly long list. Twenty names and addresses. If I'm lucky, I'll find the one with a headlight out, and in essence, our killer. Then, we'll nail the son-of-a-bitch.

See attached documentation:
Printed copy of referenced chat room discussion
February 18 – Server [Redacted]
Case# 608437

PRINTED COPY OF REFERENCED CHAT ROOM DISCUSSION

Case #608437

Date: 2/18
Chat Service: Redacted
M.K. TASK FORCE
Private Chat Room

LyDetector: Everyone! Tragic, but good news! Corin Peterson has been found!

AlibiBreaker: What?!

Private-i: Already? Where?

DoubleDHelix: Tragic? Must mean unalive.

LyDetector: News said a garbage man found her outside of a storage unit complex right off the freeway. Tossed in a dumpster. Get this... wrapped in plastic! Clean plastic.

dTECHtive has joined the chat

dTECHtive: Wrapped in plastic? That's new. The clean part, not so much.

DoubleDHelix: Yeah... plastic? Doesn't seem like our guy.

LyDetector: They're giving him credit. Fingernails were taken.

AlibiBreaker: Could be him. I need to call my brother. See if he knows anything.

Private-i: That's not all, folks. PD has updated their website. The victim's head was detached with teeth removed!

AlibiBreaker: Holy Cow!!!!!

GetUoff: Whoa!!! Definitely escalating.

LyDetector: Sorry! Typo. Clear plastic! Wrapped in CLEAR plastic! Isn't that fascinating?

DoubleDHelix: Why? Think he wants his handy work on display?

dTECHtive: You're asking why? He's a psycho! That's why!!!

Private-i: Yuck. Do you know how messy that would be?

LyDetector: Psychological. He is clearly distancing himself. The plastic must be a physical boundary he has created between him and the victim. Could be he's remorseful? Fighting guilt?

Private-i: Bullshit ideology! Sadistic Psychopaths don't have feelings! They're monsters. Stop making him human!!!

LyDetector: But why is she different? He must have felt something to make her standout from the others.

AlibiBreaker: You think? It does seem more.. intimate.

AlibiBreaker: Wrapping her up, keeping her warm.

Private-i: Shit's sake, Olive. Thin plastic wouldn't keep anybody warm.

Private-¡: You and Lydia need to stop romanticizing! He's a butcher!

DoubleDHelix: Wait! I bet she bit him! That's why he yanked the teeth!

AlibiBreaker: Ooooooo..that's an idea. I hope she took a chunk out of the sleaze ball!

GetUoff: Wouldn't stand up in court.

DoubleDHelix: What wouldn't?

GetUoff: The bite mark. Unreliable evidence. Look it up. Dozens of people have been falsely sent to jail. Sloppy prosecuting.

GetUoff: Any lawyer worth his salt could discredit the science.

DoubleDHelix: Still would be great circumstantial evidence if there were photographs of a bite mark.

Private-i: Just as much proof as bruises!

GetUoff: Compelling, yes. Jury pleasing, absolutely. Actual fact? Unprovable and a great acquittal defense.

AlibiBreaker: Is the plastic important or not? And why remove the head? That's what I want to know! Are we sure this is our killer?

Private-i: Yes, the plastic is important, Olive.

Private-i: Probably was the only thing he had around to help contain the mess. Nothing more.

AlibiBreaker: And the head?

dTECHtive: He needed more leverage.

AlibiBreaker: Leverage? What do you mean?

dTECHtive: To pry the teeth out. Probably couldn't get a good grip, but with the head detached...

AlibiBreaker: Oh, that's awful!

LyDetector: You're all missing the point! We can trace the plastic!Printed copy of referenced chat room discussion

Private-i: Lydia is right. If we can get a sample to compare. Check hardware stores, paint shops, plastic wrap manufactures.

AlibiBreaker: I'll call my brother! Maybe he can manage it?

LyDetector: Do that! Sorry, but I gotta run, guys. Need to meet a man about a car.

"Mr. Clean"

Case# 608437
Evidence# 04-291
Typed confession letter

Nine months prior to the eviction and moving into this dump, back when I still had Sophie, it all started with a form letter in the mail. Something to the effect of...

Dear Sir or Madam,

It has come to our attention you are the owner of a 3 series, 1988 BMW and may be in the market to sell. We are highly motivated buyers and would like to extend a lucrative purchase offer. Would we be able to schedule a time to view your vehicle in person? Please contact us at blah, blah, blah, at your earliest convenience.

There was no signature or name. Only a logo.
I threw it away without a second thought. Did the same a week later, and the week after that. Was mildly surprised,

when I found a similarly worded email in my spam box, and greatly annoyed, at the handwritten note stuck to my door a month later. The tone, of which, was more demanding. Insistent.

Which was weird because my car is a piece of junk. Granted, an expensive feat of German engineering, but still junk. I assumed the interested party was a collector of some sort, so I was confident they wouldn't mind it lacking modern day conveniences, like a back-up camera, GPS navigation, or Bluetooth technology. I sure hadn't. The absence of these advancements had served well to keep me off the map of society.

But the exterior? Dents, scratches, and a crumpled rear fender scarred the outside, while faulty wiring, tore-stitched leather, and a sun-cracked dash plagued the inside. A true collector would take one look and realize it wasn't the gem they were hoping to acquire and move on. Why waste their time? Besides, I didn't need the cash. Money wasn't my problem. Not yet.

The short in my right headlight, THAT was a problem. And since my more-expensive-than-my expensive-lawyer of a mechanic was waiting on a part to fix the damn thing... again... I was forced to park it in the small garage attached to my rental. There it sat, collecting dust while I either walked or took the bus to the gym, grocery store, work, ect. A minor inconvenience, though better than a potential traffic citation. I already had two. Risking another would draw the eye of my parole officer, and I didn't want that.

Which is why I didn't report the break-in. I'd jogged home from the store to find my garage door propped open with a broom stick. My car was still inside, the hood popped and doors left wide open, the trunk closed, which was a saving grace. Stupid of me to have left the garage unlocked.

Whoever had been inside, they'd left in a hurry, their job

undone, whatever that was. Had they intended on stealing the car? A few parts? Or was it a petty thief, scrounging for old CD's and loose change? Whatever the intention, it was apparent, my arrival had spooked them off. Which made me ponder. How had they known I was coming? I surmised there had been a lookout.

Nothing was taken, though the car had been ransacked. The glove box was left hanging open, the meager contents spilled out upon the passenger seat. The sun visors pulled down and askew, supposedly, the prowlers looking for a hidden key. And here my mechanic thought I'd been nuts for wanting a separate lock for the trunk. I knew what I was doing...and why.

As for the door leading from the garage to the house, scratches and grumbling growls of warning had come from the other side. Sophie sounded as if she were a hundred-pound muscled Rottweiler, instead of the twenty-pound pup she was. She'd done her job. No one had gotten inside. To be honest, I was weak kneed with relief. My place was in shambles, and I hadn't cleaned, which was why I'd gone to the store. I'd needed more bleach.

I'll admit, I had not put the over-eager appeals nor the ceasing of further requests to view my vehicle together with the garage break-in as it never dawned on me, they could be related. Why would I? I lived on the crappy side of town. Just on the border, where one block boasted nice two-story houses and middle-class cars, and the next street over, boarded up windows and overgrown lawns.

The perfect place to blend in and not draw attention. Neighbors weren't friendly or sociable. No risk of a huge block party or sidewalk yard sale. Everyone kept to themselves, outside of the occasional semi-friendly wave across the street.

Living in a rental, I had no worries of finding my next-door neighbor on my stoop with a "welcome to the neighborhood" basket of wine and cheese, or someone asking me to join their fantasy football team or book club.

It was the perfect place to hide, and I wanted to stay hidden. What I had failed to realize was I'd just been found.

TAPE IS ABSENT

Lydia

Case# 608437
Evidence# 05-4333
Recovered voice journal- Transcript- Timeline unknown

Fun fact. Breaking into a house isn't as hard as you might think... that is, with practice, and I'd had plenty by the time I found him.

Taking the list of twenty BMW owners, I whittled it down to five viable and realistic suspects. I suppose you could judge my efforts as being sexist, even accuse me of practicing agism and ableism, but the reality is, I was trying to duplicate the FBI profile.

The first to be struck from the list? Women. The likeliness of the Manicurist Killer being of a feminine nature was beyond slim. Almost zero. Next? Old men. It's doubtful anyone aged in their seventies would have the strength or stamina required. Killing is a young man's game.

Speaking of young men, I happily scratched off two high schoolers, their social calendars filled with sports practice, cheerleaders, and partying. Though more than physically capable of the terrible deeds committed, the FBI profile advised the age range to be anywhere from early twenties to late fifties. The bureau knows its stuff, so off they went. Age and sex aside as eliminators, the last two names stricken from the list were both disqualified due to physical attributes... If you haven't thanked a Veteran lately, you really should.

This left me with the final five, all aged appropriately and physically fit, differing in lifestyles, livelihoods, and relationship statuses. All happily living in a higher tax bracket than I, which isn't hard. I'm barely scraping by on unemployment. Lost my telemarketing position due to "displacement by offshoring." Greedy outsourcing bastards.

Anyway, now came the easy part, right? I mean, how difficult can it be to figure out if someone's headlight is out? All you have to do is wait until dark, tail your suspect, whose probably leaving work to head home, and as soon as they've turned on their headlights, BAM! You've got your answer. Except, four of the five didn't use their BMW as their daily driver. As for the guy that did, both of his headlights worked fine. Though the dude doesn't apparently understand the concept of dimmers. High beam jerk.

That left four guys, their vehicles under lock and key. It was Charles's idea to play to their ego and wallet. He drafted a form letter pretending to be an organization of wealthy collectors interested in viewing, and potentially purchasing their vehicle. Only one of them responded with interest. So, I gussied myself up, threw on a tight pencil skirt and low-cut blouse, and posed as an auction buyer. No dice. Everything worked fine, including his libido.

The other three were more elusive, ignoring our attempts to make contact. We tried different modes of communication, even going as far as taping the request letters to their front door, but still, no return correspondence. So, we had to take things up a notch.

In the course of justice, sometimes, things aren't always black and white. You gotta get a little grey, and thanks to having a tech guy on our team, who could hack into outside home security cameras, we were able to track the comings and goings of our suspects. After learning their routines, it was then up to ol'retired Tom, who'd seen more than his fair share of house breaks-in while working the beat, to give pointers on how to infiltrate the garages. I did my own research, and thanks to the age of the BMW series, Do-It-Yourself videos came in handy with learning how to pick the door lock and if need be, hotwiring the car. Yeah, I know how to hotwire. I'm an official badass.

There were one or two close calls, near scrapes with the law and nosey neighbors. If it hadn't been for Andy keeping watch on the hacked security cameras and warning me via text, I might very well have spent the summer cooling my heels in lock-up, while the group scrounged for bail money. And thanks to Debbie's advice.... Oh, hold on. Someone is at the door.

Sweet! UPS just delivered! Um... where was I? Oh! Not wanting to leave behind my DNA. Debbie was emphatic that I not accidentally contaminate potential evidence, so I made sure to wear gloves, and kept my hair in a ponytail, covered by a hair net, tucked up inside my ski mask. She also insisted I wear plastic booties over my shoes with my pant legs tucked within my socks. A bit overkill, but she had a valid point. Corrupting proof would only get him off the hook.

Having eliminated all but one, the last on our list lived in a less than friendly neighborhood and kept odd hours. Unpredictable, he had no set routine, nor a cemented work schedule. Though big on fitness, he chose random times to hit the gym, it open 24/7, and walked or jogged everywhere.... Which was suspicious. Why wasn't he driving at all? As for his social life, it was deader than mine, and that's saying something.

Which was ironic, because due to an obligatory family dinner... I had to spend Saturday evening with my parents for game night. I was forced to relinquish my nightly surveillance duties to Andy, who managed to hack into the doorbell camera of the neighbor across the street, and promised to send hourly updates via text.

With a quiet evening expected, this guy not being a social butterfly, it was alarming when Andy sent a 9-1-1 text. Potential serial killer guy had a date and supposedly, the two were having a "chill night in" at his place. I couldn't ditch my parents, and believe me I tried, so I was forced to check my phone every five minutes, my heart beating out of my chest in anticipation.

It was a little after nine when Andy reported the female had left the residence through the front door, departing in an unknown vehicle. Apparently, Andy had gotten up to take a piss, and upon returning to his computer, only caught the last second of her hopping into the car and its blinding tail lights. Seemingly alive and well.

I know this might sound weird, but I was a little disappointed. I was hoping we had caught him in the act. Because frankly, this guy was our last chance. If it turned out his headlight wasn't burnt out, and he was, in fact, as innocent as the others we'd verified, it meant I hadn't cast my net wide enough. By my rational, the killings were localized, so, the killer had to be as well, right? And if he wasn't, then we'd have to start all over again.... and that thought was depressing as hell.

Then again, what if she'd hadn't casually strolled out of his house and gotten into a ride? But rather, stumbled down the stairs and flagged a car down? What if she hadn't left, so much as, escaped? I had to know.

So, Sunday morning, dressed all in black, my hair up, and booties already covering my shoes... I drove myself out to his neighborhood and waited for a moment of opportunity. I'm lucky no one called the cops on me. I looked suspicious as hell.

The second he stepped outside his front door, I texted Andy and told him to pipe back into the neighbor's camera. Grainy or not, it was better than nothing, and watched as my prey walked away in the opposite direction. Once he'd rounded the corner, I exited my vehicle and jetted across the street to his place, which was in dire need of a coat of paint, and thanked my lucky stars he didn't have an automatic garage door... Though, it was heavier than shit to heft open, and I had to use a broom stick to keep it propped ajar. The last thing I wanted was to accidentally trap myself inside.

It took all of ten minutes to get in and out. The car was left unlocked, except for the trunk, which didn't have an inner hatch release. Backseats didn't fold down either. That was all secondary to my mission. I needed to get the motor running and check the headlights. I'd started to pull out my tools, but noticed a set of keys hanging from a hook by the backdoor leading into the house and thought, Bingo! Sure enough, spare car keys, and from the sound of it, Cerberus himself, standing guard on the other side of the door.

I snatched up the spares, jumped inside the beamer and thrusted the keys in, wrenching the engine over, the inside of the tiny garage lighting up... on the left side only. I quickly hopped out, verified that indeed, the right headlight was burnt, then yanked the keys out of the ignition and did a happy dance.

It was interrupted by Andy's text, warning me our perp

had rounded the corner, and would be back any second. I quickly mimicked a car prowler by ransacking the vehicle and popped the hood, leaving a little "screw you" behind. Then I returned the spare key, bolted out of the garage, and sprinted for my vehicle, spinning out of the neighborhood before he even made it halfway down the block. I seriously burnt some rubber.

More importantly, I uncovered the identity of the Manicurist Killer. Did what the cops were too inept to do. Put a name to the monster. Three, in fact: John Michael Duncan.

"Mr. Clean"

Case# 608437
Evidence# 04-291
Typed confession letter

After the incident with the garage, someone began stealing my mail. Right out of the mailbox at the end of my walkway. I put up with it for weeks. Wrongly assumed it was a neighborhood wide issue perpetrated by low life punks looking to score uncashed welfare checks. I ended up renting a PO Box down at the local Mail-N-More, which pissed me off to no end. All I ever got was junk mail... and the occasional summoning from my parole officer. Random drug tests, my ass.

Packages were swiped off my front porch as well. Mere seconds after notification they'd been delivered. Brazen little twerps. I debated on putting up a security camera, but thought better of it. The last thing I wanted was documented video of my comings and goings... even if it was for my own peace of mind.

On the topic of cameras, this was around the same time

I'd discovered the old busybody across the street had one of those video doorbells aimed right at my front stoop. A can of spray paint and a flat-head screw driver later, the problem was solved. At least, until she could afford a new one. What a shame Social Security doesn't pay more.

However, it was a good reminder I needed to remain diligent. My self-induced house arrest had produced an unforeseen complacency. A sloppiness. The effect of which, had become even more apparent with my last late-night visitor.

Advertised as discreet and rumored to be worth the exorbitant fee, I engaged a service. Not one to typically debase myself with hired help, I'd given in to my darker desires, and as requested, my ordered "date" arrived via a black town car, slinking her way into my abode.

Things progressed quickly, as is the nature of these transactions, and I was enjoying myself immensely with her company. That was, until she knocked over a glass of Merlot onto my white wool rug. I'll be honest. I lost it. Had a complete freak out, and acted very ungentlemanly. She scurried out the door to her awaiting driver, and left me behind to scour my precious rug with various cleaning agents. Nothing worked.

Not even bleach. The red stains simply wouldn't come out, so I was forced to toss the rug. Rolled it up as tightly as I could, propped it up between my recycle and refuse bins the night before garbage day, and said a little prayer in hopes the waste disposal guys would take it off my hands.

Next morning? The rug and both bins, rubbish included, were gone. Snatched right off the street in the middle of the night. They showed back up a whole month later, minus the rug and garbage, both roughly tossed onto my front yard with no explanation. I'll tell you; it was a relief. Hauling my junk to the landfill every week was quickly becoming a pain in my ass.

You'd have thought I would have clued in quicker. That I

would have put together all the odd happenings, drawn the conclusion I was being watched. Analyzed. But frankly, it was the last thing I expected. I mean, other than my parole officer, who would care what I was up to? Well, him and my financial advisor.

That's right. I'm a rich orphan. Lost my parents when I was a teenager, just shy of my eighteenth birthday. Murdered in their sleep. Guess who the number one suspect was? Though nothing was ever proven. Now considered a cold case, there hasn't been a new lead in over fifteen years. Which is perfectly fine with me. I'm too old for juvie now.

Lydia

Case# 608437
Evidence# 05-4333
Recovered voice journal- Transcript- Timeline unknown

I stand corrected. His actual name is John Michael Duncan, the third. He's got those fancy Roman numerals after his name on all of his correspondences. Even his junk mail. Very, *la de da* for a guy who gets enhancement pharmaceutical ads, body builder magazines, and supplement coupons on the daily.

Don't even get me started on his diet. The dude practically eats nothing but protein bars and kale. Stuffs enough Omega 3, Vitamin B, C, & D and other letters of the alphabet down his gullet, on top of copious amounts of creatine, protein, and whey, that I'm surprised he's not fossilized from the inside out.

He's also a bit of a clean freak. I don't know how many bottles of bleach the average person uses in a week, but I doubt four jugs is the norm. Wet wipes, powder cleansers, bubbled scrubbers, disinfectant, and formula sprays... you name it, he uses it. Which, I suppose, if one is cutting up bodies in the basement, all of the above would be required for cleanup. At least Mr. Clean separates the recycling from the trash.

Ugh. He even looks like Mr. Clean. Bald, blue eyed, and muscular. Yeah, well, that's stuck in my head now.

Let's see, what else can I tell you? Um... Oh, he's stinking rich. Sickening, isn't it? For the last month, we have been picking this guy's life apart. Ol' Tom ran a background check through friendly channels within his last precinct. Found out Mr. Clean has a record. Pleaded guilty. Of what charge? Tom's source couldn't say. Court records were sealed by the almighty dollar.

Must be nice to have that kind of influence, born with a silver spoon in your mouth. Whatever the offense, I bet any other man, with only a penny to his name, would have done serious jail time. But this guy, the Trust Fund Baby? He gets a slap on the hand, and released back into the private sector.

Not all is doom and gloom. We got the name of his parole officer. Olive's brother is willing to rub some elbows and I'm hoping he's slick enough to extract information without tipping off our competition. The more Olive talks about him, the more I worry he's not the brightest bulb, and frankly, I can't pile anymore on my to-do-plate, or my credit card.

I'm practically maxed out. The interest rate alone on cash advances is killing me, and before you start to think I don't know how to budget, it was the only way to get my hands on cash fast.

Bribing the mailman was no easy feat, let me tell you! With the threat of federal offenses, potential jail time, and losing his job, he was understandably skittish. But after waving a couple crispy Benjamins under his nose, he started to waver. He wouldn't actually agree until I told him Mr. Clean was a pedo. That did the trick. Nobody likes a pedophile. Which, our perp might be! Once we peg down his parole officer, we'll know for sure. So, I wasn't exactly lying, that I know of.

I had to dish out more funds for supplies too. Bought things like latent fingerprint kits, spy cameras, tracking tags, genetic testing kits, and.... Oh! A couple of fancy wigs! Thank goodness for Prime Deals and free shipping. Speaking of shipping, I also had to flip the bill for postage and packing on that wool rug. Sent it off to Debbie for testing. Shoot! I haven't mentioned that yet, have I?

So, a couple of days after the mystery woman escaped his house in the middle of the night? Mr. Clean threw out a rug with blood stains splattered all over it! At least, looks to be blood. It's red, whatever it is.

DoubleDHelix? That's Debbie. She studied to be a forensic laboratory analyst before she got knocked-up and decided to be a stay-at-home mom. She's got friends in the business who are willing, on the down low and for a not-so-nonminimal fee, to test the rug for us. We all had to pool our money together and send the payment to Debbie. For my share, I had to hock a few things. I tried to save some dough by suggesting I cut out and send only that section, but Debbie insisted it needed to be the whole rug. There were things, other than DNA, they'd be looking at. The blood splatter pattern, for one. She had an excellent point, and to be honest, I felt stupid for questioning her, so off the whole thing went.

I redeemed myself when I told her I managed to get a

hold of Mr. Clean's credit card statements. That seemed to impress her! I, of course, didn't tell Debbie the lengths I'd gone to go about it. She wouldn't have approved. In fact, she was only okay with the rug and garbage campaign, because it was piled up on the street corner and officially within the public domain.

Needless to say, I had to tell a little white lie, fibbing that I'd found his bank and credit card statements at the bottom of the garbage bin. Dumpster diving approved. Bribing a federal employee, not so much.

Worth every penny, though. It is amazing how much you can learn from someone just from their buying habits. Like, where they like to eat, buy gas, their chosen television streaming services, dating websites, and so on. A plethora of information just waiting to be picked through and dissected. I can almost see the way this guy thinks. Interpret what's important to him and how he values it.

Which makes what he does for a living so odd... uh, hold on. The chat room chimes are going nuts... What's everyone so... Oh, no. We've got another missing woman.... Named... Audrey Rae... Audrey Rae Collins.

See attached documentation:

Printed copy of referenced chat room discussion

August 05 — Server [Redacted]

Case# 608437

PRINTED COPY OF REFERENCED CHAT ROOM DISCUSSION

Case #608437

Date: 8/05
Chat Service: Redacted
M.K. TASK FORCE
Private Chat Room

AlibiBreaker: Guys! Just got a text from my brother! He says they've got another missing woman!

AlibiBreaker: News channels will be reporting on it shortly!

Private-i: Got a name?

AlibiBreaker: Yes! Audrey Rae

Private-i: Olive, is Rae spelled correctly? That a typo? Not RAY?

Private-i: Andy, can you find a digital footprint on the vic?

AlibiBreaker: Sorry! Audrey Rae Collins

AlibiBreaker: Rae is middle- with an E!

dTECHtive: On it!

DoubleDHelix: Did your bro give any other details or only a name?

AlibiBreaker: His texts are still coming in. One sec!

AlibiBreaker: Reported missing earlier this morning.

AlibiBreaker: Family waited twenty-four hours before going to police.

AlibiBreaker: She AND her vehicle are both missing.

GetUoff: Damn it! We're already behind the eight ball timewise. Ask him for last known location.

DoubleDHelix: Where was she taken from? Work? Home? A Store?

AlibiBreaker: Hold on, I'll ask!!

Private-i: Olive, does Lydia know? Shouldn't someone text her?

GetUoff: Her phone is out of commission. She ran out of minutes.

DoubleDHelix: Vic description? Clothes worn? Type of car she drives?

dTECHtive: Found her socials! Family is pleading for help and has listed details.

dTECHtive: Last seen leaving the dentist.

dTECHtive: Was supposed to meet up at a birthday luncheon for her mother. Never showed to restaurant or work next day. Neighbors say car not in driveway that night either.

dTECHtive: Scrolling….. Freshly divorced.

AlibiBreaker: Yes! My brother says they are looking at the ex-husband, but he's got a pretty solid alibi.

dTECHtive: Appears to have been a messy break-up. No kids, thank God!

dTECHtive: She's a looker! Appears to be in her early thirties?

DoubleDHelix: Again... Vic description? Detailed please!

Private-i: Olive? Can your brother get me a license plate number?

dTECHtive: Redhead, shoulder length, straight hair. Hazel eyes, slim build, small chested, nice ass, athletic. Caucasian.

DoubleDHelix: Last seen wearing?

dTECHtive: Family post says: blue jeans, flip flops, green top, and a light cardigan, white in color.

LyDetector has entered the chat

Private-i: Andy?… Anything about the vehicle she was driving?

dTECHtive: License# LV2YOGA, 2020 Toyota Highlander, white.

GetUoff: Wanna bet she's into Yoga?

Private-i: Good catch, Charlie! Might see if she teaches or attends classes at the same gym as Mr. Duncan... We need to establish a connection.

Lydetector: Wait! She was last seen at the dentist? Which dentist?

dTECHtive: The family post doesn't say. I'll scroll her socials and see if I can find anything. Maybe she did a "check-in" post?

Lydetector: AB, does your brother know?

AlibiBreaker: Asking now!

GetUoff: Point of order: This may not be connected to our guy. He's always left the Vic's car behind.

Lydetector: Not true. Leticia Lopez always rode the bus. He's broken this rule before.

GetUoff: Not having a car isn't the same as having a car to leave behind. Just sayin'.

Private-i: Speaking of vehicles, I believe Mr. Duncan's car is still at the mechanics, correct, Lydia?

Lydetector: Looks it.

Private-i: See! Explains why he took the girl and her wheels.

AlibiBreaker: Bro says it was Dr. Kite's Dentistry office on 10th and Lincoln Ave.

Lydetector: Thought so! We've got our connection to Mr. Clean! That's his dentist!

Private-i: How in the hell do you know that, Lydia?

Lydetector: I have my ways...

"Mr. Clean"

Case# 608437
Evidence# 04-291
Typed confession letter

I hope you didn't misconstrue my last sentence. I didn't kill my parents. I am, however, still under scrutiny, and in certain circles, maligned and suspected of their deaths.

Never officially charged, this doom of Damocles' has continued to hover over my neck for almost two decades. A constant fear in which public demand and outcry will outweigh actual proof and the sway of hearsay will result in handcuffs. As you can imagine, living under that kind of stress is damaging to a young man, even with a heavily endowed trust fund to console him.

My parents were found slain in their beds while I was as snug as a bug in mine. I have no doubt my throat was next on the agenda. The killer, whoever they may have been, having not reached me before the alarm was raised by the housemaid in the middle of the night.

It was no secret I didn't get along with my parents. My

mother was an exacting woman. Demanding and belittling, a raging perfectionist with a fetish for cleanliness. No wonder I turned out the way I did... Whereas my father, a grandiose and boisterous social narcissist, hid his malcontent for his family behind the pursuit of public office.

Too self-absorbed to raise a child properly, I was shipped off, halfway across the country, to a private school, and only brought home when needed on the campaign trail or forced by traditional holidays... such as Christmas break, and that year, Christmas break coincided with a pre-re-election fundraiser. A holiday themed Gala to be hosted at our Hampton retreat for the state's finest.

The house had been nothing but organized chaos, my mother ticking demands off her list as she berated the staff. Shouting directions and insults while whirling her way from room to room, white gloved, inspecting for a speck of dust. A place for everything and everything in its place was a Sunday hymn compared to my mother's zealous mania to be flawless. Her screeches had bounced off the vaulted ceilings while my father hid in his office, desk phone glued to his ear, scratching dollar amounts on a legal pad, thanking his wealthy donors, who hoped to be on next year's guest list.

With all the hustle and bustle, there was no shortage of witnesses to report the verbal arguments I'd had with my parents that day, at separate times and locations within the house. Both were heated shouting matches of grand proportion and one of which, led to a physical altercation. A slap across the face. I still have the scar on my cheek thanks to my mother's gaudy 16 carat ring.

Chock-full of rebellion, I snuck out the night of their demise. Headed for the beach with a stolen six-pack from our fridge under my arm. Found solace in the company of fellow teens, a group of strangers. All bitching and moaning about their woes around a campfire, drunk and high, the wafering scent of weed intermingling with the sea air.

I caught a ride back home a little past one in the morning, where I proceeded to stumble my way across the massive yard and rounded the five-car garage to the kitchen door in back. I suppose if I hadn't been stoned, I would have questioned the door being ajar, but thought it simply luck I wouldn't need to climb the ivy terrace and squeeze my drunk ass through a window.

After scarfing down a whole platter of hors d'oeuvres meant for the gala, and guzzling a half gallon of eggnog, I proceeded into the living room, where I relieved myself of my gluttony, rather nosily, and then crawled my way into my bedroom. There... I assume, as I don't recall much more, I passed out, only to be awoken by the housemaid's scream an hour later.

Questioned as to why she checked on her employers in the middle of the night, the maid confessed she and my father had a standing clandestine appointment every Friday in her room. I'd have had called her a liar, for my father's reputation alone, but her swelling belly validated her claim. My parents, for years, hadn't shared a bedroom, so I imagine she felt little fear of being caught, when she decided to instead, visit his room, surprised to find that not only was he not alone in bed, but slaughtered, his wife, inexplicably, lying beside him.

Why didn't suspicion fall on the maid? Though jealous rage is a good motive, she, nor her baby, would be the one to inherit literal millions. And in all honesty, no one believed, not even me, that the mousy maid killed my parents. But then again, I knew who arranged their deaths... and potentially mine, though maybe the plan was always to have the finger of guilt pointed toward me.

Who, then? Father's sole sibling and the only other living relative I have. My aunt.

With money potentially being of no object, I'm sure it wasn't hard for her to find a hitman. Someone willing to slip in under the cover of darkness and slice a few throats, a generous cut of the inheritance their awaiting payment. Her plan had only half succeeded, the job only half done, her nephew alive and well, reaping the benefits of her scheme.

I was, and still am, alone in this theory. As the only other relative to gain at my father's demise, minimal as it was, Auntie was spared all suspicion, the chief of police failing to investigate any possible involvement. (The two went WAY back and between the sheets.) Besides, my aunt was halfway across the country! Stuck in a snowbound airport, destined to miss the gala. How convenient.

To this day, in general caution and in some appreciation, I pay my aunt's bills, on top of a yearly allowance and a newly leased Mercedes every twenty-four months. I give in to her little demands, and still go to her home for Christmas, because that is what family does.

No doubt that surprises you, and you may be wondering, shouldn't I live in fear she'll try again to have me bumped off? Auntie wouldn't dare. I've made it abundantly clear that when I kick the bucket, all my money will go to charity. Those ASPCA commercials get me every time.

In retaliation, my loving aunt keeps the gossip mill going, quietly working behind the scenes to crucify me in the public eye. Stroking the fires of suspicion while simultaneously proclaiming her unwavering support, hoping the mass's cry for justice will prevail and someday a grand jury will indict.

One cannot legally profit from murdering one's parents, and if found guilty, as next of kin, she'd inherit my father's unspent millions. Which, I bitterly admit, is a real concern. Good thing money talks and I have much more than she.

Which brings me full circle to my finance advisor, the only person, other than my parole officer, who checks in on me. Gerardo Bertola. An old school accountant, who doesn't like digital copies floating upon the internet ether. He prefers hand written, coded missives. Very cloak and dagger, my Uncle Gerri.

That's what I like to call him. Uncle Gerri. Meant as a term of endearment, and only behind his back, never to his face. He's the closest thing I've ever had to a father figure. It's a shame he doesn't like me.

With a suspiciously crisp and pristine Power of Attorney in hand, he had leap frogged over my aunt, taking custody of me and my finances, not necessarily in that order, and claimed he was fulfilling my parent's wishes to care for my wellbeing. As my father's oldest friend and money advisor, it could have been that he clung to me as the last link to the past. More likely, to cover his own ass and funny figures. Whatever the case, Uncle Gerri took me in hand, brought me home to finish high school under his tutelage, and then proceeded to grease the palms of admission clerks who were willing to look past my poor SATs, eventually guaranteeing my enrollment in an Ivy League Pre-Med program. I was to be a doctor.

His plan, whether I wanted to be an MD or not, or even a good one, was for his ward to earn a doctorate of any kind, be it by the skin of my teeth, and set up a practice upon where actual talented physicians worked under my name. Leaving me to sit fat and lazy upon the board, laundering Uncle Gerri's dirty money behind a medical white coat and stethoscope.

I was sheltered, impressionable, and naïve to his plot. I didn't relish the idea of four years of pre-med before getting into the nitty gritty of a doctorate program, but I wanted to make him proud. Be worthy of the care that was being showered upon me... Somebody actually gave a damn.

My devotion only lasted a semester. The rest of my time was spent in joyous debauchery, frilled with blessed irresponsibility, my monthly allowance disappearing up my nose. I indulged in this new hobby and social acceptance to the point where my grades plummeted far beyond the deep reaches of Uncle Gerri's wallet. His scheme was in jeopardy and he was none too happy about it.

In an effort to right the ship and speed my schooling along, I offered to change my focus to Mortician Sciences. I thought it a good compromise, never bothered by bodily fluids or stenches, the business structure of a funeral home much like a doctor's practice. Labeled a ghoul, the suggestion was negated, and I was sternly placed back onto the straight and narrow, my monthly funds greatly depleted. In consequence, my social life devolved as well. I was once again an outcast.

Determined to re-cement myself in Uncle Gerri's good graces, I put my nose to the grind stone, and finished pre-med, all the while dreaming of the freedom my trust fund would grant me at the age of twenty-five. It was by pure chance, on a visit back home, that I stumbled across a little black ledger. It fallen, or placed, in the heat register by my father's desk. A book of figures, dark deeds, and names. The old man, not only being an esteemed Senator, was also a black mailer, payment for secrets kept listed as election donations. I was quite surprised, and elated, to find Uncle Gerri's name in the book. It seems, he'd been working off a long-standing debt... I owned him now.

This new dynamic came in handy on the second term of medical school, my pre-med days done. Accusations had been made against me, and if I hadn't had that little ledger of secrets to hold against him, I'm afraid Uncle Gerri would have washed his hands of me, and that would not have done. Guys like him, you don't let slip through your fingers.

Keep in mind, I was never under the illusion that Uncle Gerri was an honest man. I knew he was skimming money off me, but with millions at my disposal, what was a few lousy hundred thousand a year? We had a symbiotic relationship. He needed me as much as I needed him.

He became my problem solver. If I was troubled, he fixed it. If I was in trouble, he got me off. If I needed trouble, he found it, paid for it, and then made it disappear. Yes, I'm very fond of my Uncle Gerri.

Unfortunately, he's grown old. Not as quick witted as he once was. With the last bit of trouble I found myself in, he under delivered, forcing my hand to hire a legit lawyer. Who, as I mentioned before, has advised me on more than one occasion to keep my nose clean. He's a miracle worker, but not God, and barely got me out of the last scape with only a two-year stint of parole and a sealed record.

I was forced to get a job, a condition of my court allowed freedom, and fell back on my years of education. Found myself, once again, in the medical field as a pharmaceutical salesman. A pill pusher... which is ironic. That's what got me kicked out of medical school. Assigned to maintain the medication cabinet, I'd dived into the cookie jar one time too many for my own personal enjoyment. Honestly, I've never been disciplined when it comes to impulses. That's what Uncle Gerri finds so abhorrent. My lack of self-control.

Ashamed, I decided to use the first year of parole as a jumping point, build myself up from scratch, and change the trajectory... start anew. Could be, in some unconscious way, this self-inflicted sabbatical was an attempt to earn back Uncle Gerri's approval... or maybe, I was tired of being an asshole.

Either way, I stripped my existence of its lavish possessions, moved to a new city where no one knew me or the family name, and did my best to live on my newly earned income. That's not to say I lived in abject poverty. I kept the credit cards and my expensive tastes.

I also turned my focus to health, and discovered body building, a disciplined hobby, of which, I thought Uncle Gerri would approve. Routine, exercise, and a strict dietary regiment... If my mind and body were occupied, my desires and impulses would diminish, become controllable. At least, that had been my hope.

Funny how something so small can throw you off course. A bump in the road which jostles you and morphs into an open crater. A sink hole. My bump came in the form of a phone call from my mechanic. He stumbled across something he shouldn't have... just my luck.

See attached documentation:
Evidence# 04-298
North Hampton Gazette
Case# 608437

North Hampton Gazette

SENATOR DUNCAN, WIFE, SLAIN IN BED

In the early morning hours of December 10th, Senator John M. Duncan II, and wife, Whitney E. Everson-Duncan II, were found slain in the master bedroom of their North Hampton estate, the gruesome discovery made by live-in staff.

The couple's teenage son, John M. Duncan III, home for the holidays, was unharmed, his room in the opposite wing, reportedly having slept through the attack, undisturbed. This was corroborated by Tina Godfrey, the Duncan's live- in maid, and Deborah Peters, their personal chef. Authorities believe the unknown culprit used the general chaos surrounding the event's set up, capitalizing on trades people coming and going, to gain access to the Duncan's home.

This tragedy falls on the eve of the Senator's Annual Christmas Gala, a charitable event for Bone Cancer Research, in partnership with Pals and Pets, a program headed by board president, Mrs. Everson-Duncan II, and Vice-chair, Stephanie Marvos. Pals and Pets is a donation funded outreach program, enabling sheltered and adoptable pets to visit cancer patients while receiving chemo treatments.

North Hampton Police Chief Stevens declined to comment on the cause of death, stating until a concrete timeline was established regarding the horrific event and all evidence collected, he could not make an official statement at this time. Senator John M. Duncan II has served as a New York Congressional Senator for five terms, leading the charge on new legislation for stricter banking regulations and consumer protections. He also served on several oversight community panels regarding finance and economic hardships. Prior to his elected terms as Senator, Duncan II was a Defense Attorney with Hyde, Chase, and Duncan. His most famous client being famed and alleged, Mob Boss "Ruby Jack", Ruben Juliano. Duncan was part of Juliano's five-man legal team. The group successfully securing Juliano's full acquittal on all hundred and twenty counts of tax evasion, money-laundering, and racketeering.

14
Lydia

Case# 608437
Evidence# 05-4333
Recovered voice journal- Transcript- Timeline unknown

It's been three weeks and Audrey Rae Collins is still missing. Her family, according to news interviews and postings on social media, falsely believe this to be a good sign. When in fact, the hard reality is, she's likely already dead, and all it really indicates, is her body simply hasn't been found yet.

You can't blame them for holding out hope. Especially when the investigating detectives only speak of Audrey Rae in the present tense, when speaking to the press. The cowards. They must know she's been gone far too long for this to have a happy ending. And to add insult to injury, it seems Detective Miller and his partner in "not-solving" crime, Detective Pickard, still haven't managed to single out even one suspect in the Manicurist killings. They remain completely clueless to his identity, whereas little old me, has already succeeded in pinpointing Mr. Clean's personal connection to each of the victims. I'm still patting myself on the back.

I started by asking a singularly key question. Why would a silver spooned jackass need or even want a mediocre job? Let's be honest. He's not in dire straits financially and it surely isn't to stave off boredom. No, if he's pulling himself out of bed and slumming it like the rest of us poor schmucks on the daily, it has to be for a particular purpose. My conclusion? He needs a disguise.

He's a pharmaceutical rep. As I understand it, he visits various doctor offices, supplement stores, and such trying to convince the proprietors to prescribe or carry whatever miracle drug he's pitching. Every day he waltzes in, flirts with the staff, buys everyone lunch, then hands out a few hundred samples with brochures before moving on to the next office. As I figure it, this career choice allows a wolf in sheep's clothing to interact with potential victims in a very engaging and unthreatening manner. Weekly, he routinely enters their lives, slowly establishing a fluid and friendly rapport, all the while, hiding his sharp teeth, until one night, he bares them against the neck of some unexpecting and trusting little Red Riding Hood. Once I realized what he was up to, it wasn't hard to connect the dots.

Firstly, Jillian Mason, the pharmacist? Of course he'd have contact with her, they literally work in the same business. That's a no brainer. Now, Addison Morang, missing woman number two? Not only did she have a membership at the same gym as Mr. Clean, she was employed as a receptionist for a doctor's office! A spine splitting neurosurgeon, who probably writes scripts like he's giving out candy! Same would have gone for Audrey Rae Collins, last known location being the dentist office. But, as it so happens, not ONLY is her dentist in Mr. Clean's sales territory, the Doc is also his actual dentist. Coincidence? I think not!

Encouraged with my findings, I dove deeper... literally. According to the pile of mustard and ketchup-stained expense reports I'd retrieved from the bottom of Mr. Clean's garbage can... Catered lunches were ordered from the Mexican restaurant Leticia Lopez managed. He didn't even tip that well! Typical cheapskate Richie Rich.

As for Corin Peterson, the woman found in the dumpster outside of the storage unit complex? Turns out she owned a localized printing company, which, if I probed deep enough, is probably where he ordered his business cards and brochures. It's elementary, Watson.

The only connection I struggled to puzzle together, at first, was poor Charlene. I mean, how would a childless, big pharma rep connect with a small town elementary school teacher?... That is, a recently widowed small town elementary school teacher. There was only one way I could think of, and it didn't take long to confirm my hunch.

Having studied Mr. Clean's credit card statements, I noticed he had a re-occurring charge for two separate dating sites. I keyed both up on the screen, and searched for Charlene Sutton's profile. Sure enough, I got a hit on the second site, her profile viewable, though, obviously no activity for the last several months... cause she's dead. My guess? Charlene had fallen for their "find love or we'll refund" deal, and prepaid.

Now, the real question was, had she been matched with Mr. Clean? If so, there was my link! It only took Andy, our IT whiz, five minutes to hack into Charlene's profile and confirm that she and Mr. Clean not only were matched, but actually "winked" at each other. Though, as far as he could see, no one took the initiative to move things along further. That's not to say Mr. Clean didn't pursue her outside of the dating site. It is completely possible he tried to make contact. For all we know, he could have stalked her, figured out her routine, and then, when he happened to bump into her, make it seem all coincidental! He would, you know.

So, you see... not only can I connect his vehicle in the area of each victim thanks to the headlight, but I now have PROOF of his personal acquaintance with each one! It probably won't surprise you that the police still haven't utilized the prior information I brought them regarding his BMW and the burnt headlight. According to Olive's brother, they haven't even issued a BOLO to the traffic cops! It's almost like they don't even wanna catch this guy.

Which was my exact point when Ol' Tom suggested we share my new found discoveries with the 1-800 tip line. I, for what should be obvious reasons, greatly opposed, and was surprised when a very heated debate took place between the rest of the members. Eventually, it was agreed we'd wait, having convinced them it was likely the police wouldn't act on our intel anyway. Come on... Why would they want to pay out any reward money?

As far as I'm concerned, patience is key in a cat and mouse game. Once the DNA results come back on that rug I sent to Debbie, DoubleDHelix, I promise, I'll shove our proof down the throats of those inept detectives, which will prove I was right all along! Hopefully, the results won't be that much longer. I don't like the idea of Mr. Clean roaming free among the masses, especially now that his car is out of the shop. Not to fret, though! I've been keeping a close eye on him. It's like my full-time job now.

I still haven't found one. A job that is. There's been no time! If I wasn't the fearless leader of this band of amateur crime fighters and in charge of all the heavy lifting, doing the cop's jobs for them... I'd have plenty of hours to peruse the online want ads. But as it stands, I'm far too busy. Of course, my landlord and bill collectors have zero appreciation for this sacrifice of income. All they want is their money! I have a pile of collection notices to prove it... If only those tickets to the South Pacific had been refundable.

Oh, and as far as my folks, all they do is complain! The two are concerned and worried I'm keeping too much to myself. Becoming anti-social. They're convinced I'm in a depressive funk, having lost my job, after everything else that's gone on. You know... with my sister.

If only they had an inkling of the good I'm doing and the closure I'll be granting the wounded families. To say nothing of the accolades I'll receive once the Manicurist Killer is behind bars! My name will be in lights, and on the tongues of newscasters worldwide! I wonder which starlet they'll get to play me on the big screen?

As you can imagine, I haven't shared the truth of my newfound calling with my parents. For one, they are still mourning my sister, and secondly, they'd be none too pleased to know their remaining child is actively tracking down a serial killer. What parent would?

Hell, it doesn't seem to faze my team, though. They have completely failed to properly appreciate all that I do, or come close to comprehending the depths of my dedication! With each of them living hours away, some literally located halfway across country, everything falls to me. If I don't do it, it doesn't get done!

If it weren't for all the interviews, late night surveillances, and countless hours analyzing data and video... Not to mention, the close calls I've risked to gather evidence or the stretching of the law, to say nothing of my pocket book, to make things happen... We'd have bupkis!

To be honest, I feel a bit resentful. Which is probably

why I spent yesterday afternoon blowing off steam and spoiling myself rotten with a much needed shopping spree!

Oh, not with my money! No, I'm dead broke. But Mr. Clean isn't.

See attached documentation:
Printed copy of referenced chat room discussion
August 23— Server [Redacted]
Case# 608437

Date: 8/23
Chat Service: Redacted
M.K. TASK FORCE
Private Chat Room

GetUoff: Just checked the PD website. Nothing's been updated on Vic #6 for 3 days!

Lydetector: I know! It's shameful!

dTECHtive: Especially when her family updates their social "missing page" daily!

dTECHtive: BTW, no new leads or sightings posted.

DoubleDHelix: She's out there somewhere.

AlibiBreaker: Poor thing! Cold, frightened, alone...

Private-i: Dead.

Private-i: Olive, anything new from your brother?

Lydetector: Sadly, he's right. "Still missing"? Only means no body found at this point.

AlibiBreaker: I'll ask him. I feel bad always hounding him when he's trying to work.

GetUoff: Better off for Mr. C if not found. No body, no crime! Classic defense.

Private-i: Speaking of Olive's brother, and since we're all here. I have a proposal.

dTECHtive: Who do you want me to hack now? 😀

Private-i: I want to start off by applauding everyone for all of their hard work.

DoubleDHelix: Here, here! Yay, us!

dTECHtive:

GetUoff: Team Work makes the dream work!

AlibiBreaker: Yes, a great team effort! Though, my bro should get an honorable mention too!

Lydetector: It's a bit early to be celebrating...

Private-i: Agreed. However, we've gathered a lot of information, and no offense to anybody here, but as a one-time actual member of law enforcement, I think it might be time to throw a bone to the professionals.

Lydetector: What do you mean by "throw a bone"?

dTECHtive: If you're suggesting a kidnapping and plopping our perp onto their doorstep... I'm all in!

AlibiBreaker: I thought when the time came, we were going to give all info to my brother?! Is that not the plan now?

GetUoff: I'm in for a road trip! Let's cast him to the wolves!

DoubleDHelix: Too soon! What about the DNA results on the rug?! It will only strengthen our case!

Private-i: I'm suggesting we call into the tip line and give up Mr. Clean.

Lydetector: ABSOLUTELY NOT!!!!!!!!

dTECHtive: And split up the reward money?

Private-i: Of course! $25,000 divided six ways.

GetUoff: Only if a conviction is achieved. No guarantee.

dTECHtive: Less than $5,000 each. Hardly worth it.

DoubleDHelix: Then again, if the cops stumble across Mr. Clean on their own, we get nothing. I could use that money to pay down my student loans!

dTECHtive: I'm all about doing a good deed, but it would be nice to get something for all of our effort, on top of putting that piece of human compost away for life. I don't see a downside of calling it in.

GetUoff: I've got student loans myself. If you think our findings are solid enough, then, might not be a bad idea.

Lydetector: GUYS!!!! YOU CAN'T BE SERIOUS!

AlibiBreaker: Again! What about my brother? I promised we'd turn everything over to him once we got the final piece!

Lydetector: We don't have all the evidence yet!!! END OF DISCUSSION! However, on that note, how are things going with the rug results?

DoubleDHelix: I'm hopeful we'll have something within the next month or so. No promises.

Private-i: With all due respect, Lydia, I believe we've taken the investigation as far as one can with the skills and limited access to information we have. It's time to let the actual lawmen take the lead.

Lydetector: Have you FORGOTTEN I've already been to the police and they DID NOTHING! I practically gave them Mr. Clean on a platter! They've failed to do anything with that information!

AlibiBreaker: That is true! My bro says they've not even issued a BOLO on his BMW... That means Be On The Look Out.

Private-i: Olive, she gave them a description of a car, not a name. We HAVE A NAME!

DoubleDHelix: That's valid. We've connected the dots for them.

Lydetector: THAT IS EXACTLY MY POINT! And they did NOTHING. It needs to be US who bring Mr. Clean to justice! Not some slow poke team of detectives who can't get off their fat asses to do some actual police work!

GetUoff: Another point... We'll need more time to pull our evidence together to create a cohesive report. It's gonna take me a bit to lay out a future court case, because you know this rich kid isn't going down without a fight. We have to give the prosecution a fighting chance to keep this creep behind bars.

AlibiBreaker: AND my brother his promotion! He's supposed to bring our findings to his supervisor! How else is he gonna get credit?!

Lydetector: We never agreed to that, AB! He's barely done anything!

AlibiBreaker: Yet! But he will and I think he deserves SOMETHING for being under cover! In fact, if we call the tip line, we'd need to split the funds SEVEN ways, not six! He should get a cut!

dTECHtive: Seven ways! Shoot... that's practically pocket change per person! Wouldn't be worth the headache of calling it in! I vote to wait!

Lydetector: Yes! PATIENCE IS KEY! We've almost got this guy! Let's not rush to the finish line! I want him as badly as you all, and I'm sure the police WOULD appreciate MY findings, but we need to make sure whoever we give this to, they will actually do something with it!

DoubleDHelix: Are you suggesting we take everything to the FBI?

GetUoff: OR THE PRESS? I think that would be ill advised!

Lydetector: Once we have all the data, THEN we can decide how we want to play it. We TRULY need to wait for the DNA rug results! Are we all in agreement to hold off until then?

DoubleDHelix: It'll only be another month or two, maybe three. I'm willing to wait.

GetUoff: Agreed, with an amendment that if another victim is swiped, we can reopen this discussion.

dTECHtive: Bonus point? They might even UP the reward money!

AlibiBreaker: It's a yes for me and my bro. I agree, we need to hold off.

Private-i: Fine. It was just a suggestion.

"Mr. Clean"

Case# 608437
Evidence# 04-291
Typed confession letter

What did he find? A tracking tag magnetized to the engine block. I'd given a nervous chuckle when my mechanic asked if I knew it was there, and then lied. Ribbed him I was worried he and his grease monkeys were taking my piece of shit car out on joyrides. He laughed, and said he'd have my ride ready by the end of the week, then hung up, leaving me to wonder... Who the hell was keeping tabs on me?

I found it unlikely to be Uncle Gerri, modern technology not being his style, and highly doubtful it was Auntie, a tracking tag too low brow for her tastes. She'd rather spite me by spending my inheritance on a pricey private dick with an open-ended expense account. She's classy like that.

Which left my parole officer... Mikey. An overworked, under paid prick, who loves nothing more than pulling my ass in for "random" drug tests. I always come up clean. My secret? I stay off street drugs. My other secret? I take steroids when not in competition and pay a kid at the gym for his clean urine. I keep it frozen and stock piled. That way, when called in, I defrost, store it in a condom like a ballon, and keep it snug against my junk to maintain body temperature. Works every time.

My lawyer parted the Red Sea when cutting my deal, and since I was considered a high-risk repeater, it was expected I do a lengthy stent of jail time. Ten, the minimum. Twenty, max. Instead, I walked out without even an ankle bracelet. Paying a small judgement in compensation to the plaintiff and a very hefty fee, the later, deposited into a Swiss bank account, owned by the honorable and corrupt judge who presided over my case. Two years' worth of parole and Mikey ended up being my only punishment. I'd count myself lucky, if I hadn't paid so much for the pleasure.

Still, it didn't figure my parole officer would be keeping tabs on me with a tracker, even if he didn't agree with the court's leniency. He's a dick to me, because he's a bully, and not because I got away with something he feels deserves a stricter form of punishment. He's just not that guy.

Another thing? The placement of the tracker. Far from an ideal spot, you'd typically wanna put something like that inside a wheel well or slid in between the backseats where stale fries go to die. Better yet? Cut a thin slit and slip that sucker under the vehicle's carpet. Trust me, they'll be none the wiser.

Where you don't want to put a plastic tracking device is on an engine block, which will grow hot once the vehicle is driven. If I hadn't had my car towed to the repair shop from the house, I'm sure, instead of a plastic tag, my mechanic would have discovered a welded, cluster of melted plastic. Whoever placed it on my vehicle either didn't understand thermodynamics and phase transition, or they were in a hurry.

Like a lightning strike, my mind zig zagged to a broom handle bracing my garage door ajar, my car ransacked, and the engine hood, unexplainably, popped. Someone had not only broken into my garage, but they'd left a little present behind. But for what purpose? Who had I pissed off?

The answer to that question (sort of) came a week later after I got my car back from the shop, minus the tracking tag. That had been flushed down the toilet shortly after I paid my bill. This bit of rebellion must have pissed off the stalker, because when I was done working out at the gym, and returning to my vehicle in the parking lot, I found it had been vandalized. The word PERVERT written in large letters across the hood, trunk, and the driver's side door in shaving cream. The passenger's side? It only read PERV... I honestly don't know if they ran out of time or shaving foam, but it still conveyed their declaration clearly.

As you can imagine, I desperately tried to wipe and scrape the lather away before anyone could see, but found myself too late, the gym's immense windows providing a clear view of my panicked antics. The only thing I could do, was throw myself behind the wheel and find the closest carwash. It did no good. The shaving cream had etched into the paint, the words still there, large, yet faded. PERVERT or PERV, depending on which side you were on.

I returned to the gym the next day to speak with the manager, a cocky ass with blinding veneers which outshined his crisp and white logoed polo shirt. Asked if he wouldn't mind looking at the security tapes, my vehicle vandalized on gym property. Told him I needed a copy for the police report and my insurance. Not that I was intending on filing a complaint or claim. Too much of a hassle. Rather, I wanted to see who had set themselves upon my path and pay them a visit... to clear the air.

It did cross my mind the culprit might, in fact, be a

member or employee of the gym. I wasn't exactly popular with the ladies. Not that it was entirely my fault. Yoga pants, cleavage popping sports bras, and ass hugging Lycra shorts were mostly to blame. I'm a sucker for flushed cheeks, soft skin sheened with sweat, and thin tank tops, which show off goose pimpled tits when the AC kicks on... I may have been caught staring once or twice, my gym shorts doing nothing to hide my excitement.

My suspicions were heightened, and potentially proven correct, when the manager explained that for some inexplicable and unknown reason, the security cameras covering the parking lot had all been turned off for the duration of my two-hour workout. He apologized profusely, though not sincerely, and said he was stumped as to how it could have happened. He was baffled, but I had a pretty good guess the next day.

Usually greeted by a friendly, albeit fake smile, the cutie at the front desk seemed too pleased to inform me that they were out of clean towels... yet, the next patron was handed two. I then approached the juice bar, and tried to order a protein smoothie, the long-armed ape behind the counter giving me a shit-eating grin... The blender was broken. I spent the remainder of my workout, eyes set on their reflections in the mirror, and watched as the front desk handed out a plethora of clean towels, soundtracked by the background whirl of a working blender, the juice bar giving away free samples.

I was now confident about how the parking lot security cameras had been switched off, but I couldn't picture Biff and Buffy, being the ones to vandalize my car. The flow and demand of clients at both the front desk and juice bar, too time constricting. They were likely complicit. However, not the masterminds, and I couldn't dismiss the vandalization and garage break-in as mere coincidence. That's not to say, I let them off the hook for their participation. Word of advice? When retaliating, always have a scapegoat.

A few Saturdays later, Biff left Buffy's apartment to find he had four slashed tires, the word CHEATER gouged into his paint job, while Buffy's little black Honda was decorated in red paint, HUSBAND STEALER scrawled in large print. Biff's estranged wife got the blame, their marriage on the skids, gym gossip swirling that the two B's were knocking uglies. As planned, all three were too busy pointing fingers at each other to realize I'd reckoned my revenge.

Scores settled, I turned my focus to the mysterious ring leader. Whoever they were, not only had they damaged my paint job, but they'd destroyed my reputation at the gym. The few "friendships" I had cultivated, even if placated out of social politeness, eroded in front of my eyes. My body building pals began to shun me, breaking gym protocol and refusing to even spot me when lifting. Their good-natured jabs, and unasked for advice, replaced with posturing grunts. Their jaws and muscles twitching in judgement, itching to cave my face in. Even the kid who sold me his urine wouldn't look me in the eye.

Even worse? Nobody asked me any questions and no one wanted my side of the incident. They'd already made their assumptions. What's that saying? There's no smoke without fire? Thus, the accusation had to be true in some context. People don't vandalize a stranger's car with vicious, false allegations.... It's just not done! Oh, but it is, and it was just the start.

See attached documentation:
Evidence# 04-295
Repair Invoice
Case# 608437

INVOICE NO #01854

DATE: 09/13

CUSTOMER: J.M. DUNCAN III
BMW 3-SERIES

DESCRIPTION	QUANTITY	PRICE	TOTAL
RIGHT HEADLIGHT- REPLACEMENT	1		$74.99
OIL CHANGE			$175.00
OIL DISPOSAL			$10.00
TOW FEE - PER MILE	9 MILES	$4.75	$42.75
STORAGE FEE	21 DAYS		$100.00
MECHANIC FREDDY	4 HOURS	$200.00	$800.00

PAID
VIA MASTERCARD
APPROVAL # 7321

REMARKS:

FOUND ON ENGINE BLOCK-
PLASTIC TRACKING DEVICE-
NOTIFIED CUSTOMER AND WILL
SHOW IN PERSON BEFORE
REMOVING.

SUBTOTAL	$1,112.74
TAX	$91.24
DISCOUNT	$0
TOTAL	$1,203.98

120 S. 1ST AVE. · PARKING ON 3RD STREET IN BACK

16

Lydia

Case# 608437

Evidence# 05-4334

Recovered voice journal- Transcript- Timeline unknown

When I started these little confessional recordings, my hope was to provide, beyond a shadow of a doubt, solid proof of guilt. Given freely by me, this evidence would be employed for future prosecution efforts, a gifted hammer head of justice to drive the final nail into a well-deserved coffin. Of course, respect and notoriety would be a welcomed form of gratitude, along with knowing I'd done a good deed... and I guess, that should be award enough. To know justice has prevailed. Except, I've come to realize, I'm not as humble as I thought. I desire fame and all of its trappings!

Fame is worthless if all it gives you is a blinding spotlight, yet, nothing flashy to wear underneath it. And frankly, I want to sparkle! If I surrender these hard sought findings, it will indeed bring me glory, but no money, and your girl is as broke as a joke.

However, if I were to take these recordings and write a memoir... Well, I could have both fame and fortune! The timing would need to be just so. I'd hate to release any information before a conviction. But once Mr. Clean is found guilty on the selective proof I'll provide to the courts, then the world will be privy to how I discovered, found, hounded, and ultimately, if I remain one step ahead, captured the Manicurist Killer.

Imagine my words and deeds climbing the best seller's lists, juicy details coyly spilled, my rivalry with the police revealed, my triumph celebrated. Not only will my clever brilliance be showcased, but the incompetence of the detectives will be uncovered. They will be publicly ridiculed, judged on the lives they could have saved, if only they'd taken me seriously.

Sure, I'll have to play my cards right. Come up with some guarantee from the publishing company to make sure my revelations don't cause me harm. Possibly, have the memoir written by a ghost writer? Their words thought to be nothing more than grand embellishments. Truths, half-truths, full blown lies, it'll be no never mind!

All that the gossip loving public will really care about is how a monster was brought to heel! Besides, no one who has spilled their boisterous deeds in a tell-all book, ever pays for their past sins. Fame, and by gone days, make them untouchable!

As for being a current nobody and my present wrongs? Complete opposite. I don't even want to imagine what would happen if I were to admit to bribing a federal employee. But! Give it a few years and some stardom?

Nobody will even care! And that's not even the worst thing I've done!

You ever see those fun, almost gameshow-*esque* questionnaires that people fill out and re-post on their social pages? Harmless, funny questions such as, What's your favorite color? Ever been arrested? Have any tattoos? What's your favorite food? Ever been out of the country? What hospital were you born in? Best movie ever?

Those "fun" questions are usually intermingled with, Name of your favorite pet? What year did you graduate? What was your high school mascot? What was the street you grew up on? What was your mother's maiden name? What city was your first apartment in? Favorite sports team? Year you were born? What's your zodiac sign?

Now, think about this! If you've forgotten or need to reset a password for a website, be it banking, credit card, or an email account, what kind of security questions are asked, to verify it's you who's requesting the change of information?

How about...

What was your high school mascot?

Have you ever lived at one of the following addresses?

What is your pet's name?

What is your favorite sports team?

What is your mother's maiden name?

And if a fraudster, intent on assuming false identities, sees the silly, fun answers you've left to float aimlessly upon the internet, well, you've given them ample information, with little to no guess work to accomplish their mission.

Your date of birth? Easy. You answered the questions...

What year were you born and what's your zodiac sign?

It's not hard to narrow the date down, especially if they also have your mother's maiden name... and the hospital you were born in. Easy, peasy with Google.

How do I know this is how it happens? Well, before my

piece of shit employer outsourced my entire section to India, I was the supervisor over their customer service fraud department. Yes! I was one of the calm and friendly voices taking panicked calls, quickly reassuring that the fraudulent charges would be immediately credited, and a new card placed in the mail in three to five business days. Oh, it was such a cush job.

I also learned a lot about bending the rules, or rather, how others worked the system, and well, since it is the credit company's fault I'm now practically destitute... Listen, what I'm about to admit to is morally righteous, completely justifiable, and assuredly deserved, but also punishable up to ten years, and as a cherry topper, an astronomical fine of $250,000 per count.

However, desperate times require desperate measures. With my rent two weeks past due, prepaid cell phone out of minutes, and my gas tank empty, my poor piggy bank was exactly that, poor, and all due to the pursuit of Mr. Clean! It only seems fair, he pay his fair share.

Andy, if he knew what I was up to, I think, would be proud of my hacking skills. In no time flat, with Mr. Clean's trashed credit card bill in hand, I reset the password to his account, changed the billing address, and opened an additional line of credit, the card being shipped directly to me, via a new PO box... and all under five minutes.

Am I fearful of being found out? Nah. When a guy like that has an open credit limit which would challenge the national debt in zeros, you know he's not checking his balance for overtures. And what if he did discover a second account was fraudulently opened under his name? Likely, he'd call the 1-800, make a big stink resulting in everything being zeroed and closed down, his life returning to normal. No big whoop. Meanwhile, until he does discover it, I plan on shopping my little heart out! I've earned this and I don't feel guilty in the least.

You know who SHOULD feel guilty? Olive's brother. For being a useless twat! He had ONE job and failed miserably. All I asked him to do, besides keeping his eyes and ears peeled, was to snag a sample of the plastic, the clear sheet that Corin Peterson was wrapped in, before it was sent off to the FBI. Said he didn't have access to the evidence room. When I pointed out, that at some point, it must have been kept in Detective Miller's messy office, and THAT, should have been his window of opportunity... He told Olive I grossly misunderstood police protocol. That he couldn't just waltz into any office he wanted to, unnoticed and unquestioned.

Well, I suppose that would be the case if he was unprepared and obvious about it. But the guy works in the file room... THE FILE ROOM. All he has to do, the dunce, is grab a file and head for Detective Miller's empty office. If questioned while searching the man's desk, all he need say, as he holds up a FILE, is, "Oh, found what I was looking for! This needs to be returned to the FILE ROOM." I mean, it can't be that hard!

As you can imagine, Olive worded these suggestions in a much kinder way than I. Thankfully, he took my advice and managed to swipe a few documents from Detective Miller's desk and made copies, then returned them, all undetected... thanks to my guidance. I swear, if it weren't for me, this shit show would run itself into the ground.

I am going to kindly assume Olive's brother didn't have much time to peruse the litany of documents that were probably splayed all across Detective Miller's desk, and that he basically just grabbed the first couple of sheets he could lay his hands on, because otherwise, I'll go insane with frustration. If it had been me, I would have made a straight beeline for anything to do with the FBI or related to toxicology and DNA... Instead, he grabbed a statement from the ex-husband of the latest victim, Audrey Rae Collins, and a few incidentals reports. Nothing earth shattering.

The only thing that struck me as informative in the ex-husband's account, was he mentioned a car, the headlight out. Funny... Doesn't that sound familiar? Think the cops will issue a BOLO now? Doubt it. But that's okay. There's more than one way to skin a cat.

See attached documentation:
Printed copy of referenced Suspect Statement
- Typed
Daniel Jay Collins, August 10
Case# 608437

DANIEL JAY COLLINS INTERVIEW

INTERVIEW STATEMENT

Case#: 789-BA
INTERVIEW SUBJECT: Audrey Rae Collins, Missing Person
INTERVIEW STATEMENT GIVEN BY: Daniel Jay Collins, Ex-husband
INTERVIEWER: Detective L. Miller, Self
Interview Start: 3:00 P.M.
August 10th

Mr. Collins, as requested, came willingly into the station to answer questions regarding his ex-wife, Ms. Audrey Rae Collins, being reported missing by family members, (mother and sister). Stated he'd not seen or been in contact with Ms. Collins since their last interaction in person, which was thirteen days prior to her suspected abduction.

He volunteered that the last interaction was at their house- previous joint residence, currently in her possession. He had swung by to drop off his set of keys and pick up his remaining items stored in the garage, their divorce now final. Mr. Collins said the exchange of keys and property was peaceful, despite the new girlfriend waiting in his car, and that it only lasted roughly fifteen minutes.

He did mention that Ms. Collins, before noticing the girlfriend and cutting their discussion short, had asked if he'd let himself into the home two days prior. Mr. Collins stated he had not. When asked why she was inquiring, Ms. Collins shook her head and frowned. In his opinion, she seemed doubtful of his sincerity.

Ms. Collins then stated it was odd that she found items moved or missing from within the residence, but did not give specifics. She also stated she'd been followed home a few times after work, referencing a vehicle with a burnt out headlight. Mr. Collins, concerned for her wellbeing, had begun to ask for details regarding the make and model of the vehicle in question, in addition to a description of the driver, if any, when his girlfriend, identified as Amanda Patterson, proceeded to honk the horn. She was apparently impatient with their friendly discussion.

This outside interaction resulted in a curt goodbye, and Ms. Collins returned to the inside of her home and Mr. Collins to his vehicle, leaving the area. Mr. Collins, at the time, had the impression that Ms. Collins, being his ex-wife, was passive aggressively accusing his girlfriend, Amanda Patterson, of being the culprit in the suspected housebreaking and car stalking. Which, he found utterly ridiculous.

When asked for his whereabouts on the day of Ms. Collin's disappearance, Mr. Collins readily volunteered proof of an alibi via pictures on his cell phone, in addition to time stamped correspondences via text messages to family and friends. He was at the Graceland Wedding Chapel in Las Vegas, getting married to Amanda Patterson, the new Mrs. Collins.

I have asked Mr. Collins to please contact me, if he later recalls anything else.

Interview end: 3:30 PM

"Mr. Clean"

Case# 608437
Evidence# 04-291
Typed confession letter

I've maligned a fair share of people, and like a skipping stone across water, those hurts have a ripple effect. Scars, which not only mar the individual, but those close to them. Family, friends... lovers. I could understand their desire for revenge, and to be honest, it felt odd to be on the other side of someone else's vendetta. To be the hunted, instead of the hunter.

It wasn't the norm for me to get my hands dirty, as I did with Biff and Buffy. Usually, when I had a problem, a micro aggression that needed addressing, Uncle Gerri was put to task. Two cinder blocks and a heavy link of chain later, my "problem" would be sinking through murky depths, forever to swim with the fishes.... Or at least, that's what Uncle Gerri insinuated would happen if they keep their shit up.

A whiz with knots, handy with a shovel, and quick with his fists, Uncle Gerri has always been a force to be reckoned with, even in his late sixties. The scariest thing about the old man? He knows people... very bad people and where they've buried the bodies. I asked him once, why he and his "friends" hadn't chosen methods of disposal that would obliterate evidence, such as lye, caustic acids... or a wood chipper.

The old man looked me dead in the eye and said, "Kid, always know where the bodies are. How else you gonna avoid the death sentence?"

That was his sweet way of pointing out a lawyer needs a negotiation tool, that is, if his client wants to avoid the electric chair. Wise man, my Uncle Gerri. But not exactly warm and fuzzy.

It had been my idea to slink off to the suburbs, to embed myself in a new life, forcing some type of metamorphosis. A plan which Uncle Gerri had whole-heartedly approved. I felt, if I were to rely on in-grained habits, go back to depending on the old man to rescue me, I'd be devolving, instead of evolving.

I decided to tackle the issue on my own and set about creating a list of people who hated me. Everything from slights to assaults, right down to lawsuits and no contact orders. It was really fucking long. You'd have recognized a name or two, one of them being Charlene Sutton.

I was obsessed with her.

Much like half the town. Her tragedy held the entire community hostage for almost a month, the salacious details used as a top of the hour draw for all three local news channels. Tag lines like: "Murder suicide, widow mourns cheating husband and best friend, details at eleven," and "Family of slain husband blames wife for refusing divorce, more after this commercial." Like a moth to a flame, I was glued to my television, enthralled with the chaos that had been Charlene's life.

She had discovered, after seven years of married bliss, that her husband was entangled in a hot and steamy affair. His mistress, an elementary teacher at the same school as she, a Lindsey Lawson, aka, Miss Lawson to the kiddies.

The revelation had been a nasty blow for more than one reason. Set to celebrate their wedding anniversary, the couple had made dinner plans, but Charlene's husband was forced to cancel. He swore he couldn't make the reservation due to car trouble and was stuck on the freeway waiting for a tow. Not wanting to ruin her evening, he suggested she call a friend and turn the romantic dinner date into a girl's night out.

Charlene decided to forgo his suggestion and headed back to the school, intent on grading papers over a carton of sweet and sour chicken with a side of fried rice. There, unexpectedly, she found her hubby and Miss Lawson, the two lovers intertwined atop *her* classroom desk.

Initially, there was talk of divorce, but Charlene, a good and forgiving soul, insisted on marriage counseling first, refusing to file. It worked, and her repentant husband agreed to end the affair. In return, Charlene pardoned his indiscretions and promised not to report Miss Lawson to the school board.

In lieu of bowing out with gratitude and allowing the couple to mend their marriage in relative peace, Miss Lawson doubled down. Unwilling to relinquish Charlene's husband. Instead, she inundated the man with lipstick-stained love notes, provocative texts, and emails. Found excuses to contact him at work or play, showing up at random, feigning fortuitous encounters.

Charlene ignored these desperate attempts. Assuming her intention of transferring schools at the end of the year and the decision to put their house up on the market, to be clear indications her marriage had withstood Miss Lawson's onslaught. That her efforts to re-enslave Charlene's husband had proved futile. Still, the woman persisted.

Eventually, Charlene was convinced that the only course of action would be for hubby to confront his ex-mistress and give the poor woman closure. According to police reports, the two ex-lovers met at Miss Lawson's home, and after having a final fling between the sheets, the broken-hearted woman pulled the trigger on him, and then herself. Classic, if I can't have him, she can't either.

Shattered by the murder suicide, Charlene took off the rest of the school year to grapple with her grief and shame, overwhelmed when the underbelly of her private life was publicly exposed to the community. Leaning heavily upon friends and family, with the school board's approval and encouragement, Charlene decided to return the following year. Back to teaching third grade, and to her realtor's disgust, choosing to pull her house off the market.

After a short, albeit socially appropriate amount of time, her mourning abated, Charlene attempted to dip her toes back into the dating pool, and that's where our paths crossed. She'd come upon my dating profile, and to my utter delight, sent me a "wink"... meaning, she liked what she saw, and was interested in learning more.

I returned the flirtatious gesture, but found her profile disabled two days later, no further communication between us having taken place. I felt cheated.

I mean, the state she was in... freshly widowed, aggrieved and alone in the world, meant she'd be easy picking for a charming manipulator. The uncertainty of her future, a practical, pheromone. Her fragile self-esteem, irrational shame due to her husband's rejection, an enticing aphrodisiac. Her mental state of confusion and mis-placed guilt for another woman's selfish act, a siren's call. Sure to attract gaslighting empaths in droves. Yes, a woman like that could fall in love or prey, to just about anybody, and that somebody should have been me.

Due to unrelenting news coverage, images of the Sutton's home and cross streets, their vehicle parked in the drive, precious clues were provided. Enabling me to track Charlene down and eventually map out her route to work. My purpose in doing so? If we could no longer cross paths on the internet, then I'd arrange for us to bump into each other in real life.

I had done my best to stay two car lengths behind, Charlene unaware of my presence, and followed her to work, forced to run several red lights to keep on her tail. Tired of keeping my distance, and aware that the next block over would bring us too close to a school zone, I utilized my aggressive driving skills. Weaved my way through traffic, managing at the last second, to merge into her lane, my taillights illuminating her frustrated frown, clearly visible via my rearview mirror.

My attention divided between the road and my quarry, I slowed in anticipation. Charlene had a very unsafe habit of applying mascara while driving. The second her attention was momentarily distracted, I slammed on the brakes, creating a chain reaction, her car plowing directly into my rear fender. She's lucky she didn't lose an eye.

As if kismet, our hazards lights blinked in unison, and I approached her vehicle, doing my best to look harmless. She appeared shaken and shocked, wary of me, probably expecting a belligerent ass. Which was fair, as she had been the one to run into me. But I greeted her with concern and kindness, inquiring if she was well, and then reassured that no harm had been done. Because, well, these things happen. I also took partial blame and explained I'd stopped short to avoid an imaginary dog who had run in front of my car.

After checking out the superficial damage, we exchanged information and swapped insurance cards. I then wished her a good day, and directed her safely back into traffic, before climbing into my own vehicle. That's how I got her number.

I texted the next day, asking after her health, and received a token response, a few hours later, gratitude for my concern. I waited two more days, then tried again, this time inquiring if she'd heard from my insurance company? The response was short and sweet. YES. I tried to keep the exchange going, suggesting it might be better if we handled things ourselves in an attempt to avoid higher insurance costs. Recommended a nice coffee shop we could meet at. She declined, preferring the insurance company handle the issue, her car already in the shop. I then offered to be her personal taxi, this nice gesture met with a resounding, NO, THANK U. She stopped answering my texts after that.

Charlene Sutton, my overtures of friendship rejected, had not been at all as I expected. I had anticipated meeting a sweet, kind hearted, people pleasing personality. A gentle, trusting soul, eager for validation, only too grateful for my attentions, enamored with me as much as I was with her. Talk about a letdown.

She ended up being a stuck-up bitch, and I had absolutely no qualms when I instructed my lawyer to slap her with a catastrophic injury lawsuit. That's fancy talk for whiplash. The case never made it to court, Charlene having gone missing. She was eventually found... and well, back to the present moment, I then decided to scratch her name from my long ass list. Dead women can't seek revenge.

See attached documentation:
Evidence# 04-211
Charlene Sutton, Cell Phone Transcript
Case# 608437

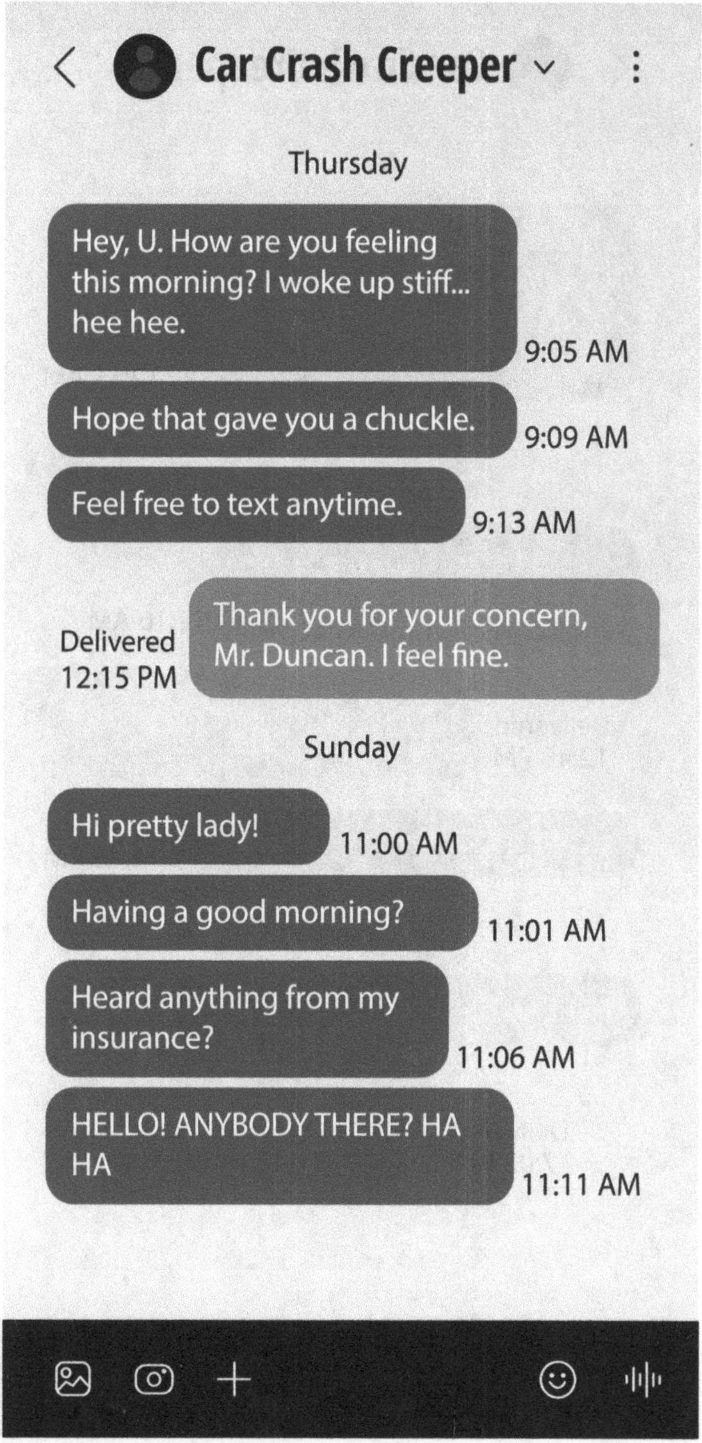

Car Crash Creeper

Thursday

Hey, U. How are you feeling this morning? I woke up stiff... hee hee.

9:05 AM

Hope that gave you a chuckle.

9:09 AM

Feel free to text anytime.

9:13 AM

Thank you for your concern, Mr. Duncan. I feel fine.

Delivered
12:15 PM

Sunday

Hi pretty lady!

11:00 AM

Having a good morning?

11:01 AM

Heard anything from my insurance?

11:06 AM

HELLO! ANYBODY THERE? HA HA

11:11 AM

Car Crash Creeper

Just finished my workout. Gonna head out soon. Gotta feed these muscles. Like to meet for lunch?
12:55 AM

Delivered
12:15 PM
YES

Great! How about the Sub Shop on 4th?
12:16 AM

Delivered
12:45 PM
SORRY! YES TO INSURANCE. NOT TO LUNCH.

No worries! Maybe next week?
12:46 AM

Monday

Hi BEAUTIFUL! Got a second?
7:00 PM

Delivered
7:02 PM
Regarding the insurance claim? Yes.

Ha! Ha! Great! I was thinking, why don't we resolve this little fender bender between ourselves?

7:03 PM

Cut out the middle man?

7:03 PM

Who needs higher insurance rates, am I right?

7:04 PM

We could discuss over coffee? I'm buying!

7:05 PM

Delivered
7:10 PM

I'd prefer to go through insurance.

Come on, FREE COFFEE... I don't bite.

7:11 PM

2 HARD! Bahahahaha 

7:11 PM

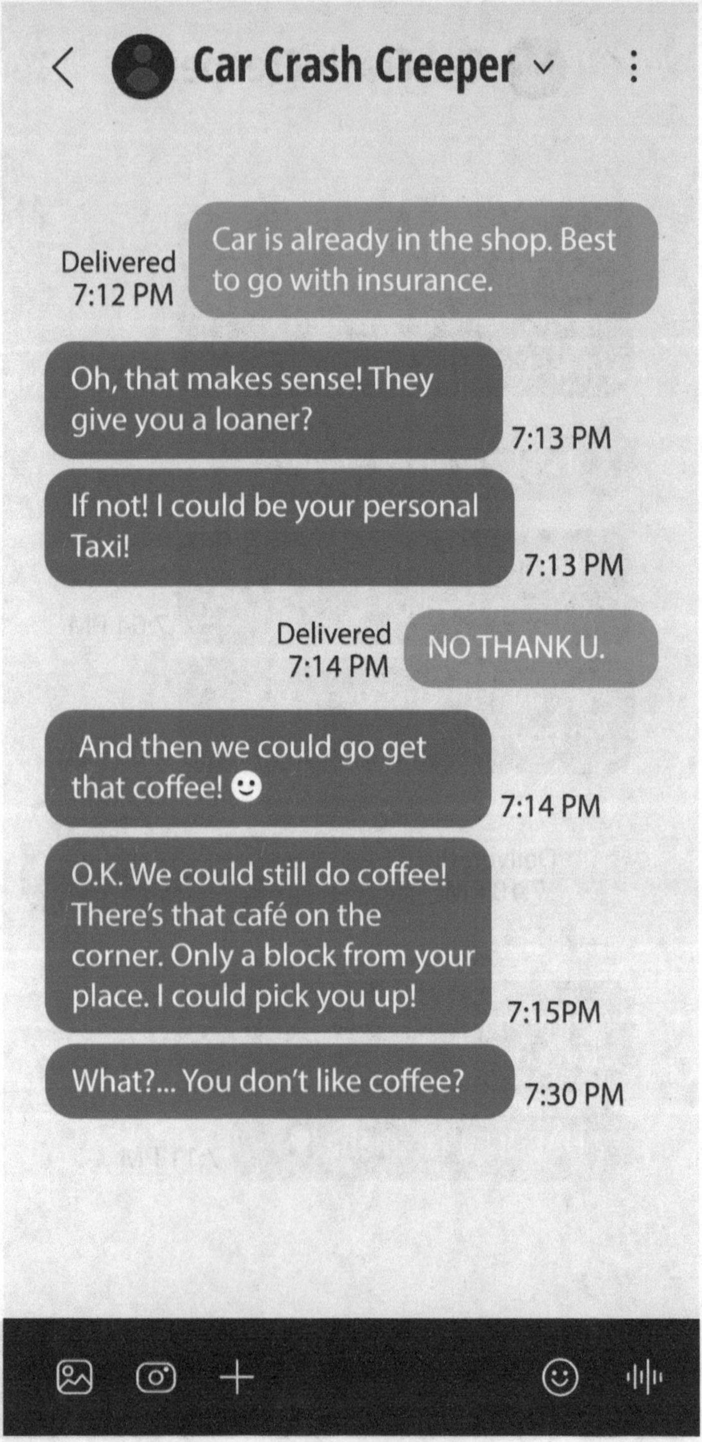

Car Crash Creeper

Car is already in the shop. Best to go with insurance.
Delivered 7:12 PM

Oh, that makes sense! They give you a loaner?
7:13 PM

If not! I could be your personal Taxi!
7:13 PM

Delivered 7:14 PM
NO THANK U.

And then we could go get that coffee!
7:14 PM

O.K. We could still do coffee! There's that café on the corner. Only a block from your place. I could pick you up!
7:15PM

What?... You don't like coffee?
7:30 PM

You could at least respond. RUDE.

7:40 PM

Are my texts not coming through?

7:50 PM

You must be busy… Text when you can! 😉

7:51 PM

Tuesday

Sorry, for the late text. I'll be free tomorrow to chat and meet up. You must have had a busy day.

1:05 AM

Friday

Expect to hear from my lawyer.

2:00 PM

STUCK UP BITCH!

2:01 PM

18

Lydia

Case# 608437
Evidence# 05-4334
Recovered voice journal- Transcript- Timeline unknown

Cadaver dogs found the body of Audrey Rae Collins this afternoon.

Even though I knew this day was coming, it's still sad news. Even sadder, was the fact that they'd found her by accident. Yeah, accident. I had assumed a search party, officially conducted by the police or her family members, had stumbled across her body, but it ended up being some lady and her two pups in training.

The chatter from the police scanner said the HRD handler... um, that stands for Human Remains Detector, had taken her doggos out to an old cement gravel pit, it located on the outskirts of town, to practice and run off steam. I guess she'd placed several scent tubes throughout the facility, some buried, others left out in the open. The majority were distraction scents, that's, uh... what they call the decomposing smell of dead animals, which normally would be something a dog would happily roll in, having the time of their life. However, with cadaver dogs, they need to learn to ignore those kinds of distracting smells, in order to locate the specified scent of human remains. You'd think all dead things would smell the same... apparently not.

The first time I experienced cadaver dogs during a recovery, I'd found it to be a bit of a letdown. I had assumed when they alerted to a scent or found the actual corpse, that the dogs would go berserk. Howl, or fly into a series of intense, high-pitch barks. Maybe even claw at the ground or run in circles, their snouts nuzzling the remains in exuberant excitement. They didn't do anything remotely like that!

Rather, after given the search command, they had put their sensitive noses to the ground, their tails swaying behind them as they picked up speed, tracking the strengthening scent. When one of the dogs alerted it'd found the source, it just calmly sat, looked back at its handler, expectant of a reward, and then patiently waited to be released. Perfectly content with a "Good dog!" pat, before being ushered away, making space for law enforcement to do their thing.

Putting the lack of theatrics aside, ... Well, that, and that someone died, it was pretty impressive to watch them work.

Anyway, this handler lady finished setting up at the gravel pit, and when she let her dogs out to train, they broke out in a dead run, straight into a section of the quarry where there were a bunch of no trespassing signs. Having taken the posted warnings of legal prosecution to heart, she'd avoided that area, the scent tubes placed in the opposite direction.

When both dogs ignored her recall and didn't return, she

excused their misbehavior as over excitement. Grabbed their leashes from her rig and quickly followed. It was a short chase.

Behind a mountain mound of pea-size gravel, both dogs had come to an abrupt stop, their tails wagging, tongues lolled. At their feet, lay the body of Audrey Rae Collins.

I won't go into all the gory details, as there isn't really anything new to report. She'd been treated the same as the other victims, minus the plastic cover, her corpse still intact, teeth and all.

I broke the news to my team, all of them having already accepted her fate, and then proceeded to give additional bad news. Mr. Clean had found the tracker I'd put on his car. That, or it had fallen off, destroyed in the process. Either way, all I got when I opened the app was a blinking disconnect icon.

Panicked, I'd thrown myself in the car and flew over to the mechanic's shop on first avenue, praying I'd find his BMW still sitting in a bay or parked out back, behind the chain link fence. Not there. Jetted over to his rental next. With the sun starting to set, the house sat dark, and after a solid fifteen minutes of no movement from inside, I risked hopping out and yanking up his garage door. Empty.

The next logical place to check was the gym. I tore into the parking lot, taking a speed bump at twenty. You should have seen it! Sparks flew from the undercarriage, and I careened into a parking space, just in time to watch Mr. Clean exit his vehicle, open the trunk, and take out his gym bag. He'd done it in such a casual, every day, kind of way, that... I don't know... I just suddenly felt the unfairness of it all.

Why does this man, this walking demon, get to continue to carry on without a care, living his life with no repercussions. Happy as a clam! Yet, women that he's captured and killed, will never know the joy of... anything! How is it he is allowed to roam among us so freely?

I'll tell you how! Because the police are cowards! They're so worried about due process and burden of proof, that they chase their own tails! It's bullshit! Meanwhile, women are dying. Correction, women are DEAD! And if the folks in blue can't or won't do what's right, then it's up to me. And what do I think I can do? Not much physically, honestly. Being 5'3, and a buck twenty-five. But, mentally? A hell of a lot.

Watching that wolf in sheep's clothing stroll into the metaphoric pasture, probably intent on plucking his next lamb, I realized I needed to rip away his false fleece. Ostracize him from the flock and inflict social isolation, marking him for the beast he is. I was halfway across the parking lot before I even realized I'd gotten out of my car.

My fury carried me up the gym stairs, through the glass doors, and up to the front desk, where a perky blonde stood, a hand placed flirtatiously on the bicep of a musclebound Adonis, wearing a Juice Bar t-shirt.

Five minutes later and a litany of lies told, swallowed whole by Barbie and Ken at the front desk, I found myself back outside, unconcerned with the parking lot's security camera capturing my next move. With a used can of shaving cream, courtesy of Ken, I proceeded to use Mr. Clean's car as a billboard, and with each letter foamed, I tore the anonymity from his fake façade.

Labeled a pervert, the beast was now marked. All beware.

19

"Mr. Clean"

Case# 608437
Evidence# 04-291
Typed confession letter

That's not to say, their memory doesn't haunt you.

The words, FOR THEM, had been scorched into the front lawn of my rental, the vandal having used some kind of herbicide or quick-release fertilizer. The two words, though cryptic, were much preferred over the defamatory remarks left on my beamer, and I was grateful it had not been a repeat performance. However, my landlord was none too pleased.

He had driven over to see the damage himself. By his red face and shaking fists, I could tell he was livid. Outraged his tenant had apparently done something to have brought wrath upon his property. Though, in my defense, the lawn was shit already, infested with dandelions and clover.

Fearful of being evicted on the spot, I spouted some excuse about, "Kids these days...," and tried to put the blame on the gang of punks who hung out at the end of the cul-de-sac. His furtive glance towards the lawns on either side and across the street, told me he didn't buy it. The only house on the block to have been targeted, mine. My offer to re-sod the lawn smoothed things over.

My tenancy on shaky ground, I immediately went to work on digging up the burnt, weed patch of a lawn, my efforts leaving behind a large square of dirt. It did nothing for the rental's curb appeal.

Trying to slap lipstick on a pig, I figured a few potted plants, and a fresh coat of paint for the front stoop, might alleviate the abandoned house motif I had going, and headed to the store. I never gave the errand a second thought.

Until two weeks later, when a manilla envelope was slid under my door, several glossy 8 x 10 black and white photos inside. The subject matter? Me and a shopping cart, perusing the aisles of my local hardware store.

A snap shot of the register at checkout was the showstopper. I appeared to be in the midst of retrieving my wallet, a shovel in my other hand, as I stood by the shopping cart, it filled with a large roll of plastic. Balanced on top of said roll, was a machete, and at the bottom of the cart, stored on the wheel rack, a bucket of lye and a bag of cement.

Let me start by stating, the photoshop skills on these images was laughable. Clearly done by a novice. That is, for the exception of the shovel. It looked pretty legit. In actuality, I'd been holding a paint extension pole, which they'd morphed into a digging spade. For the rest of the carted items, they'd used cut out images from the store's website. The sizing was all wrong and the wired cart was warped, bent around the oversized roll of plastic, the photo clearly edited. The machete sitting on top was a nice touch, though.

My humor quickly dissipated with the realization someone had taken it upon themselves, to not only follow me around with a camera, but to doctor photos, which for some reason, were felt to be damaging towards my character. This was evident by the black Sharpie scrawl on the back: "STOP OR ELSE."

Or else, what? The assumption was that copies would be sent to the authorities. Though what they'd do, other than laugh themselves silly, was beyond me. However, the implication of the photo said more than I wanted. Clearly, it was insinuating I'd done or was planning to do harm to someone, using the "purchased" items as aids of disposal. As if I'd ever use lye... Was I an amateur? Uncle Gerri would roll over in his grave... if he were dead.

Clearly, they didn't know who they were dealing with. And yet, I had a feeling they did. Knew exactly who I was and what I'd done. What I didn't understand, was the timing. Why now? And most importantly, which one? Who, was this mystery person avenging?

The message burned into the lawn, supposedly offered the answer. All of "THEM". But, unless you cared about one, you wouldn't care about the others. So, which "one" was the catalyst?

I went back to my long ass list of names. So many wrongs. All of them worth vengeance in one degree or another, and then I realized... You only seek retribution on the behalf of others, if they, themselves, cannot. This person sought justice for someone incapable of doing so themselves.

That shortened the list... a little.

Meanwhile, my life had to go on. The requirements of my parole demanded it, with eight months still beholden on my debt to society. And it wasn't my fault if somebody out there thought I owed a heftier pound of flesh. If the harassment continued, whether I liked it or not, I'd be forced to pull Uncle Gerri out of retirement. Make the ol' man handle it. I had other things requiring my attention.

One of which, was an upcoming Men's Physique body building competition. I'd signed up months ago, and though I was tempted to not show my face, after what happened at the last gym, I'd worked too hard not to compete.

There was another motivation as well, but I'm not ready to talk about her yet.

See attached documentation:
Evidence# 04-211
Bob's Hardware and Garden
Receipt Copy
Case# 608437

BOB'S HARDWARE AND GARDEN
825 South 5th Street
Springfield County
Hours: Mon.-Friday 7:00 A.M-9:00 P.M.
Sat.-Sun 7:00 A.M.-10:00 P.M.

10/05 4:02 PM

CASHIER: HALEY C.
Terminal: REG#3

Transaction ID: #e6d597ef
Type: CREDIT

                    SALE

Number: xxxxxxxxxxxx0048
Entry Mode: Swiped
Card Type: Mastercard

8543209 $19.99 x2 $39.98
6" POTTED "SUMMER DAYS" FLOWERED PLANTS

4589300 $24.99 x1 $24.99
4FT-6FT FIBERGLASS EXTENSION POLE

4583890 $9.99 x1 $9.99
PAINT TRAY, METAL, DEEP LINER

6284181 $14.99 x1 $14.99
3 SET, PLIER KIT, COMFORT GRIP

3720900 $28.98 x2 $57.96
WEATHER SHIELD, PORCH & PATIO LATEX
FLOOR PAINT

Sub Total   USD$ 147.91
Sale Tax   USD$ 12.12

Grand Total   **USD$ 160.03**

                 CUSTOMER COPY

               Thanks for supporting
                 local business!

                   THANK YOU

Lydia

Case# 608437
Evidence# 05-4334
Recovered voice journal- Transcript- Timeline unknown

Unfortunately, in my anger, I completely forgot to attach a new tracker to that hunk of junk beamer. Took me a whole week and half to tack on another, and that was slapped onto his loaner car. Mr. Clean's BMW? Oh, it's currently in the shop awaiting a new shiny coat of paint. Thanks to Moi!

The downside to my impetuous act of revenge? The sneaky sneak has wised up. Instead of parking in a darkened alley, or on some obscure side street like normal, he's taken to parking directly under parking lot lights or in handicap spots. Doesn't even have the decency to fake a limp. Jackass.

I had to do an army crawl across a busy grocery store

parking lot just to tag the loaner! Almost got ran over by a little old lady, who mistook me for a speed bump. And believe me, scooting flat on my belly and elbows over a gum wad, oil pooled, and God-knows-what grimy parking lot, was not my first choice.

Originally, I tried to sneak back into his garage, it being far cleaner and safer... albeit, a hell of a lot creepier, but shithead, apparently has installed a new automatic garage door opener. Any future hope of infiltrating his place is now completely dashed! Which sucks, because I really want in that house!

Oh! And another thing? The man-eating Cujo which I had feared would tear through the flimsy fiberboard back door of his house? Yeah, turns out it's an ankle biter. Well, calf biter might be a better height description, but it's still a far cry from the hell hound I had imagined. It's an ugly little thing too. Charcoal grey, with a snubbed nose, and bat ears. Ohhh, what are they called? Leticia Lopez had one... Hold on, gotta Google... Oh, yeah. A Frenchie. French Bulldog. Frankly, I don't get the appeal, but then, I'm a cat person, so...

Back to the point. With Mr. Clean being off his digital leash, I could not, in good conscience, let him roam untethered around town. With him no doubt being back on the prowl, I took it upon myself... because who else was gonna do it?... to stalk his every move.

Confession? I loved every second. That's not to say the sight of him didn't curdle my stomach, but the thrill... The challenge of being undetected? To be within feet, if not, mere inches. Close enough to touch, and yet, he not be aware that my presence wasn't destined by pure happenstance or simple serendipity? But, rather, my will.

It was like a drug, and each day, I chased the high. How close could I get? Dare I lock eyes? Physically engage with the enemy? Risk speaking? My bravery wouldn't have been so bold, if not for the slew of disguises and personas I'd developed, so as to hide in plain sight.

Not to say, there wasn't trial and error. In the beginning, I over did it. Eagerly swan dived into the expensive and brand-new finery which now fills my closet to the brim. Played around with colors, discovered I was more of a summer than an autumn. Mix and matched Gucci with Dior, accessorized with Prada and Versace, and strutted my stuff in Christian Louboutin.... all courtesy of Mr. Clean's credit card.

I spent a near fortune on makeup as well. Viewed hours of beauty tutorials, learning how to apply fake lashes and contouring, completely changing the shape of my face and nose. Oh, and wigs! I had a blast experimenting with all the shades of color and varying lengths. It was amazing how drastically they transformed my entire appearance! One day, I'm a cute girl with a bobbed cut, the next, straight hair past my ass. By the time I finished getting ready each morning, I was staring at a completely different person... and she was smoking hot.

Which meant I needed to change my strategy. Looking that delectable would only draw the sleazebag's eye, and really, what I needed to do was blend in. Be visible, but invisible. So, I traded couture for a pair of comfy sweats and a hoodie, but kept the wigs. Wasn't too broken up about losing the high heels either.

Even after all that, there were times, my presence was not probable. That no matter how I looked or dressed, I would be notable. After all, traipsing in and out of each doctor's office on his sales route would have been a bit obvious. The work around? A fancy, hi-tech camera with a super-duper telephoto lens. You know... I keep thinking I'm gonna eventually hit the credit limit on that charge card, but it hasn't been declined yet! Anyway, having a camera allowed me, from the relative safety of my car, to peer straight into any building with windows, and when I say any building, I mean his house. I guess you might say, I'm a bit of a voyeur... I'd say, I'm a lot of one.

Stakeouts at his place have become my guilty pleasure. I wait until the sun goes down, and under the cover of darkness, park across the street. Then roll down my window, the fall chill buffeted by my car's heater, and take aim.

Some of his windows have blinds, and others, sheer drapes, all except the basement windows. Those are curtained with a thick, black material. Both too small for someone to crawl in or out, I find it suspicious they're draped at all. The nights he disappears into the basement, doing who-knows-what, I allow myself a little shut eye, knowing he'll be down there for hours.

However, the nights he plops down in front of his computer... It's safe to assume he's utilizing the wide web to troll for his next victim. The guy spends hours, and I do mean, hours, scrolling a multiple of social media and dating sites. "Hearting" this, "liking" that, "winking" at some girl he doesn't have a chance in hell with... He's all over the place. I make sure to keep a running tally, zooming in as far as I can, and snapping photos when he's paused too long on a pretty face.

It's in these moments, that I feel the most helpless. Despite all my efforts, one of those young women will be his next victim, and why? Because without someone new being taken, we won't have the opportunity for him to make a mistake. He's been too clever, too careful, too meticulous. The hope, which I know is sickening, and something I hadn't understood in the beginning, is he'll become cocky, sloppy, make a mistake, and that's when I'll be there to catch him in the act.

Unless... he can be warned off.

See attached documentation:
Evidence# 04-428
Nick's Camera Shop
Receipt Copy
Case# 608437

134182

NAME _Lydia Lawson_   DATE _Sept. 15_

ADDRESS ______________________ PHONE ______________

CITY __________________________ ZIP ________________

E-MAIL ____

QUANTITY	DESCRIPTION	AMOUNT
1	Nikon Z9 mirrorless Camera SN 3003632	4,499.99
1	Nikon Nikkor Z 600mm f(4TC VR S Lens	13,499.99
1	Camera Bag - Leather	1,299.99
1	Camera Tri-Pod	379.99
	Pd in Full Via VISA ENDING in 9321	
	SUBTOTAL	19,679.96
	TAX	1,613.76
	TOTAL	21,293.72

20 DAY REFUND/EXCHANGE POLICY
MUST BE IN ORIGINAL CONDITION

"Mr. Clean"

Case# 608437
Evidence# 04-291
Typed confession letter

As it so happened, there wasn't a need to summon Uncle Gerri out of retirement. He volunteered.

The ol' man had been reviewing my quarterly investments and expenditures, no doubt siphoning the accumulated interest, when he stumbled across a series of automatic payments. The lot being deducted from a seldom used checking account. It typically reserved for laundering suspicious funds, the string of "unauthorized" payments applied to a newly open credit account, the balance quite substantial.

The discovery had warranted a phone call, the old man's voice booming, "Shit, Kid! Run out of dollar bills?"

Convinced I'd set out to impress some tart, my manhood wrapped firmly around her pinkie, Uncle Gerri proceeded to rip me a new asshole and demanded to know the stripper's name. It was clear any ground I had recovered in trying to earn back a semblance of his respect was now completely lost. I couldn't blame him for the assumption, considering my history. That, and some of the purchases he'd rattled off... Designer handbags, colored wigs, six-inch heels. Shit, I wouldn't have believed me either.

Still, I persisted in pleading my innocence, and swore up and down I hadn't paid for companionship via free reign of a credit card. Rather, I argued I had been targeted by a dark web scammer. A cyber charlatan, who used my personal information, probably leaked from some hacked server, to help themselves to my money, or rather, Uncle Gerri's. Purely random... right? The old man didn't buy it either.

"Come on, Kid... Who in their fucking right mind defrauds a credit card company, then makes sure they get paid? Only a shit for brains would set up automatic payments for stolen goods!"

I disagreed. I thought "Shit for brains" was quite clever.

Not only had they opened an additional account under my name without detection, they'd ensured the spending spree could continue by making sure I flipped for the bill as well. It was just their poor luck, they'd tapped into one of Uncle Gerri's "special" accounts and unwittingly, woke the dragon.

Reminiscent of a fiery serpent protecting his horde, the old man flew into a financial rampage. Shuffled money from one financial entity to another, liquidating businesses as he hopscotched between currencies, leaving nothing but zeroed accounts in his wake.

As a result, the ill-gotten funds, now sunk into diverse holdings spanning different time zones and languages, had become temporarily inaccessible. And though our tracks were well and truly covered, Uncle Gerri thought it best to implement a strict allowance. Instructing any money outside of my meager paycheck was to be left untouched.

It was lousy timing. I hadn't had a paycheck in over two weeks.

Coincidentally, my employer had received an anonymous tip in the form of a mailed letter. The accusation as damning as the photographic evidence which accompanied the claim.

I'd been accused of selling the company's pharmaceutical samples for cash. Derelict bums and street whores supposedly my "customers". I was immediately placed on an administrative leave pending investigation... unpaid.

Funny enough, I wasn't concerned I'd lose my job, though I probably should have been as the un-doctored, glossy 8 x 10 offered as proof... Well, it HAD captured an exchange. A young man and I standing beside my car's open trunk, cash in hand, the case of samples clearly in view... Except the tipster had it all wrong. I'd been the purchaser, not the seller.

On top of that, the snitch claimed the samples sold were pain killers, whereas I dealt in cardiovascular agents. Heart products. Everything from anticoagulants to blood pressure to beta blocks and so on. Not exactly the kind of goodies that would appeal to opioid druggies or meth heads.

Regardless, until H.R. had finished their investigation, I was destined to be penniless, left with a lot of time on my hands... and you know what they say about idle hands.

22

Lydia

Case# 608437
Evidence# 05-4334
Recovered voice journal- Transcript- Timeline unknown

Oh, my goodness!... I just pulled off the most EPIC PRANK!... Oh, hold on, hold on. I gotta get out of the parking lot before he comes out of the store... One sec.

Alright, car's Bluetooth is connected... OH. MY. LANTA! I cannot believe it worked! Yes! OH... I'm just soo... Okay, okay. Get a load of this!

Dang it! I don't think I've updated in a while. Let's see... Ummm, I'll start with his job!

Mr. Clean doesn't have one anymore! Got busted for trafficking drugs! YEAH! He hasn't reported to work in at least three weeks. Which means, the little birdie who squawked to his employer about Mr. Clean's dirty dealings, has succeeded in getting his ass FIRED! Sooo, good job, me! I was the little birdie!

Truth be told, I caught him BUYING drugs, not selling. But that doesn't matter. The photo I captured, combined with the anonymous mailed letter, portrayed a different version. One, in which, his employers bought stock and barrel! Kicking his ass to the curb, like the trash he is!

In the big scheme of things, it might not seem that huge... It's not like the guy needs a weekly paycheck, but it's a win because as I've mentioned before, he uses his nine to five as a way to rub elbows with would-be-victims. Meaning, I've put a plug in the potential prey pipeline... in person, that is. He's still heavily active on the internet, WHICH brings me to now!

I happen to know Mr. Clean has a hot date scheduled this afternoon with a poor, naïve, unsuspecting chick he's been chatting up on the web... One of many, I should add. They have plans to meet for a cappuccino, which seems to be his go to suggestion for all first encounters... and always the same coffee shop. It's an attempt, I'm sure, to come across as non-threatening. Proposing a neutral space for the first face to face... a public setting... inexpensive, yet sophisticated... plus, taking in mind, almost everyone has a caffeine addiction.

Oh, but, what a shame he's not gonna make it to his date! Yeah, no... He'll be spending the rest of his day sitting upon the porcelain throne. Hell, he'll be lucky to make it home before he shits his pants! OH... I was so slick! You should have seen me! I slid up beside his cart at the grocery store, and with one swift movement, exchanged his Americano for another, one laced with my dad's left over GoLYTELY colonoscopy laxative, and then I just walked away!

He was so entranced with the pretty, young thing handing out cheese samples, he didn't even notice when I squeezed past, my fake pregnancy belly sticking out a mile wide! Completely oblivious, as I cut over to the next aisle with HIS coffee in hand! Oh, man! That drink is gonna hit him like a ton of bricks... and then he's gonna shit bricks!

Which also means, I get a night off! I have spent EVERY EVENING parked in front of his house, playing peeping-Tom through his windows, and let me tell you, there are several, late night, lit by monitor-glow "moments" I wish I could wipe from my memory!... Wonder if I can do a switch-a-roo with his hand lotion, like I did today with the coffee?... Then spike it with poison ivy or maybe substitute it with hemorrhoid cream. He'd walk funny for at least a week! Hmmm... Something to think about.

Anyway, tonight, I plan on curling up on the couch with a glass of Merlot and watching an episode of—

<<Recording paused>>

Sorry, got a phone call. That was mom... checking to see if I still planned on picking up flowers for the cemetery on Sunday. It's the anniversary of Lindsay's death. Two years, in fact. Mom insists we should visit and place flowers on her grave as a family. But I already know it'll only be Mom and me. Dad won't go.

He mourns Lindsay as if she died yesterday, but then, she was always his favorite. The apple of his eye. The stroke to his ego. Taking more after him, than mom. Dad never found fault in anything she did... at any age. Not even when she split from her spouse, which was all her decision... Rick, that was her husband, had been completely blindsided.

High School sweethearts since sixteen, Lindsay suddenly declared she was having an identity crisis and felt they needed time apart so she could "find herself"... Dad, of course, swooped in and said she could move back home... rent free.

Told her she married too young, and insisted, she should see a bit of the world, then splurged on a mini-summer vacation for her and mom.

That left Dad and me at home... So, while those two were off gallivanting, doing their utmost to take Lindsay's mind off her troubles, he and I were left to pack up my sister's life. I gathered the cardboard boxes and packed her belongings, leaving Dad to handle the legal side of things.

Never having thought Rick good enough for his little princess, Dad gleefully hired a divorce lawyer on my sister's behalf. Instructing the attorney to have papers drawn up, ready for her return, more than happy to place the blame of the failed marriage at Rick's feet... then, eventually, a few weeks later... at mine.

It had started innocently enough. Dad had sent me to pick up the last of Lindsay's things, where from there, I was supposed to drop them off at the storage unit. I arrived at their old apartment, and when I knocked, Rick answered the door, red-eyed and heartbroken. Like a lost puppy, he looked utterly destroyed and... and well, I'd always had a crush on him. A fact Lindsay was fully aware of when Rick asked her out on their first date. And I suppose, I still held a flicker of a flame and a helluva grudge.

But that's not why I went back the next day... or every day after. These secret visits to his apartment started as sympathetic gestures of comfort, but quickly transcended into long-desired, nightly passions. Where, whirlwind or not, we soon found ourselves falling in love. We even talked of eloping and jetting off to a tiny little island in the South Pacific, home to an all-inclusive resort... That was until Lindsay came home from vacation... early.

Succeeding in "finding herself," Lindsay had realized she liked being Mrs. Rick Baker... and was only too horrified, as were Mom and Dad, to discover her baby sister had slid into the marriage bed she'd abandoned.

Lindsay begged Rick to take her back, but he was torn... undecided. He felt after all their years together, he owed it to their marriage to try and make it work, yet, he'd rebounded. Found warmth, acceptance, and a willing lover in me... In the end, he told each of us he needed time to figure out his feelings... then proceeded to dump us both.

It didn't matter. To my parents, Lindsay was the only injured party. Not Rick, and surely not me... the backstabber. And a few months later, when my sister's affair with Charlene Sutton's husband came to light... Well, how could my parents blame her for going off the deep end after my betrayal? Could anyone, after what I'd done, expect Lindsay not to fall apart? Wouldn't they excuse her low-self-esteem, throwing herself into the arms of a married man, as a cry for help?

Lindsay wasn't a homewrecker! Not like me, who was given no quarter to the fact Rick and my sister were legally separated, that she'd rejected him, and had moved out and on, taking back her maiden name... No, her actions... her selfish reasoning, her obsessive delusion was all my fault!

And they were right... If only I'd been a good sister. A good person. Maybe Lindsay would still be alive, and Charlene Sutton would still have a husband... If only.

Well... We all have regrets, but unlike my sister, I can do something about mine.

23

"Mr. Clean"

Case# 608437
Evidence# 04-291
Typed confession letter-Undated

Then again, not having a forty-hour work week allowed more time to focus on my physique, the amateur body building competition days away. I was in the cutting phase, meaning my intake needed to be limited, which included liquids. Restricted to a diet tailored to dispense of excess body fat, my only beverage of choice was electrolyte infused water... I would have killed for a beer.

Early mornings until roughly late mid-day were spent in the gym, lifting and running cardio, with sessions in between dedicated to practicing form. Flex poses in the mirror, perfecting my routine. In the evening, after a bland meal of boiled chicken and tofu, Sophie and I would take a trot around the neighborhood, then it was back down into the basement, pumping iron until my limbs were jelly. I was dedicated, disciplined, and for once, happy.

Life seemed to be on the uptick. For starters, I was taken

off suspended leave, set to return to work the following Monday. The anonymous allegations brought against me proven unfounded, the investigation closed. In addition, the stalking and harassment had come to an end. This I attributed to Uncle Gerri. Supposing the old hound, having given chase, had followed the digital trial to our tricky rabbit, where he snapped his slobbery jaws of retribution upon their jugular, the rabbit no more... I doubted, whoever they were, would bother me again.

Which also meant, I needn't worry about my vehicle being vandalized, traced, or broken into any longer. A relief, as I hadn't relished the idea of risking the new paint job out in the open.

In fact, I had asked my mechanic if I could borrow his loaner for a while, deciding to keep my BMW safe in his care a few weeks longer. He was a pal and said it was fine. Even waived the lot fee, and when I finally picked up my BMW, I noticed he'd had his shop guys detail the inside. It was almost like having a brand-new car.

I suspected he felt bad for a kindred soul... When I had brought the beamer in, PERVERT etched into the paint, I half-expected to be asked to take my business elsewhere. Expecting he would jump to the conclusion, as others had done, that the branding was warranted, a declaration of fact. But as it turned out, he'd clamped a hand onto my shoulder, gave it a firm squeeze, then tossed me the loaner keys, mumbling under his breath, "Bitches will be bitches."

It was nice to have a friend.

Another positive? My dating profile was suddenly drawing A LOT of attention. I figured it was the algorithm, an update to the app. Nothing else had changed. I didn't think too much of it. Life was on the upswing, and I was eager for some company... I found it in spades. However, I was wary it would be fleeting. Competition is fierce in the dating world. One minute you're hot, the next, you're not, so I was quick to talk myself up.

Bragged about my weight lifting and how I drove a BMW... though I purposely neglected to mention the model year. Sprinkled in a few white lies among my boasts, hoping to impress. Like, how I'd won my body building competition... I hadn't. Or that I was head of sales at my job, instead of just in sales, and that I was currently on the market to buy a house, new to the area and forced to rent a temporary place.

I felt no shame in this, as I wasn't looking to find "the one". Nothing so deep. I just wanted to get laid by a nice girl... I was tired of women who had been traded back and forth like baseball cards. Not to mention their cost... way too pricey for the new budget.

I met a few "potentials" for coffee... and only coffee. Never seemed to make it to the next date, and sometimes, that was by my choice. Most times, by theirs. I'll admit, I was growing frustrated... and realized, I needed to change my tactic.

The women I conversed with, they were my age, early thirties. Established, confident, and selective. They already had careers. Some, homeowners. All with a strong sense of their own self-worth, and too quick to see through my bull-shit lines. Which meant, if I was going to have any chance at scoring, I needed to lower my sights... seek out a more achievable woman. Someone innocent. Naïve to the ways of the world... and preferably... men.

I baited my hook by adjusting my profile, the new answers more attractive to a carefree younger woman. Ensured, that the tone was purposely repulsive to anyone seeking mean-ingful commitment, hopefully repelling those that were looking to settle down or find their happily ever after... I wasn't their man. I was all about having a good time. Attending concerts, bar hopping and travel. Made sure to hint at my good fortune and generous wallet, having the good sense not to actually use the term "Sugar Daddy"... though, it was implied.

I was a little nervous at first, when the tidal pool of interest immediately dried up. My net cast, I feared perhaps trolling in younger waters might have been a mistake... After all, a few flirtatious nibbles were better than none. I had been worried needlessly as messages began to trickle in, the tide of opportunity rising... All that was left, was to reel one in.

Funny, how I ended up being the one to get snagged on the hook.

I had been sifting through profiles when she popped up on the screen. A busty blonde holding a beer bottle, it pressed against her sultry lips, her bright smile partially obscured. She had "winked" at my profile, in addition, to sending a simple DM of, "Hi, Handsome!" followed by two heart emojis.

I pounced on her profile and clicked through the photos, scrutinizing each one... I'll admit, I was being cautious. Leery of being catfished, fooled by another fatty who understood the importance of photo angles. I was relieved to find the pictures consistent, a few full body shots included. She was pretty... not gorgeous, but above your average plain Jane. Assuredly within my league.

I returned her gesture and quickly perused her info.

Twenty-one, community college, pet lover, and "not looking for anything serious"... Which was EXACTLY what I was looking for.

I quickly Googled her name and found a plethora of information from one of her social media accounts. It showcased her interests, allowing me to quickly find something we could "bond over", along with additional photos, displaying a more provocative side... poses showing a little bit of shoulder here, some cleavage there, even a nice shot of her legs... Her face wouldn't launch a thousand ships, but her hour-glass figure sure could.

Realizing I wasn't the only man on this dating app that would soon discover this treasure trove of wanton desire, I replied to her message with a simple "Hey, Beautiful! You've got a gorgeous smile."

A volley of compliments began to bounce between us as we flirted over the next week, chatting here and there until she felt safe enough to propose we meet... I let her be the one to suggest coffee, but made sure I picked the café, choosing a place close to my house. It needed to be... My headlight was out again.

See attached documentation:
Evidence# 04-341
March 02 Amber Alert
Haley Clark>>
Case# 608437

AMBER ALERT!
SPRINGFIELD COUNTY

MISSING
Haley Clark

MISSING SINCE: Last Friday, 03/02

MISSING FROM: Springfield City, Springfield County

AGE: 17

SEX: Female

RACE: White

HAIR COLOR: Blonde (Pink highlights)

EYE COLOR: Hazel

HEIGHT: 5'5

WEIGHT: 130 lbs.

AMBER ALERT: The Springfield Police are looking for a missing child: Haley Clark. Haley Clark is 17 years old, white, female, approximately 5 feet and 5 inches, weighing 130 lbs. She has hazel eyes and dark blonde hair with pink highlights.

She was last seen at a local coffee shop meeting with an unknown male who she left with on foot.

If you have any information or see Haley Clark
PLEASE CONTACT 9-1-1

Lydia

Case# 608437
Evidence# 05-4334
Recovered voice journal- Transcript- Timeline unknown

Should I tell you the good news, or would you rather hear the bad news first? Ha! Yeah, well... Since I'm actually only talking to myself, might as well go with the bad news... and spoiler, even the good news isn't that great.

DoubleDHelix sent me a private message. The damn rug STILL hasn't been tested! It keeps getting bumped down the line and shoved to the side... out of sight, out of mind! The lab's excuse? "Requests for expedited testing on official cases takes precedence." What a bunch of crapola! I mean, don't these people understand this isn't about some random bank robbery or a solitary death? We're dealing with a serial killer, who will just keep on killing! This needs to take top priority or the body count will continue to rise! And haven't they heard of the concept of working OVERTIME? Skip your damn lunch hour and get the rug testing done! It's no wonder it takes decades for cases to be solved! You know what else? They had the balls to suggest things might speed up if we sent more money... Oh, man! Talk about being a day late and a dollar short!

Yesterday? I wouldn't have blinked an eye at the veiled extortion. Would've simply whipped out Mr. Clean's credit card and said, "Name your price!" But today, when I tried to buy groceries, the card was declined. Which means the jig is up, and I'm back to being impoverished... I suppose, I could sell some stuff online, like the fancy purses and couture clothing. But I'll have to try to hock the rest at the local pawn shops, which I hate, because they never give the true value of anything... the crooks.

Oh, but that's not all the bad news.

Sunday, while Mom and I were placing flowers on my sister's grave, she collapsed. Scared me to death! The doctors said she suffered a minor stroke... and thankfully, would make a full recovery... which is the good news. However, after she was released from the hospital, to be on the safe side, I ended up spending a couple of days at my parent's place.

Now, while that is indeed bad news, it gets worse. While playing nursemaid to my poor mother, Mr. Clean decided to return his loaner to the body shop and pick up his BMW... which isn't tagged with a tracker.

And that still isn't the bad, bad news. What is... is that I hadn't realized he'd made the switch until THREE days later! Which means, three whole days have passed without him being monitored. No record of where he's gone!

I had been so distracted with taking care of mom and catering to dad... who, at the age of sixty-five, is still incapable of making his own damn sandwich!... I mean, my mom waits on him hand and foot! It's like she's his personal frickin' maid, and heaven forbid she were to croak tomorrow, the man would probably starve to death! Sorry!... Getting off subject.

All of that to say, I was too distracted to notice the icon for the tracker was blinking at the wrong location. I thought the car was sitting in his garage. Not at the repair shop! So, out of pure spite and not wanting to go through the hoopla of attaching another air tag, I took a crow bar and smashed in his right headlight... Which needed to be done anyway! Because everything I've told the cops, and all of the information I've collected, says that our guy... Mr. Clean, aka, the Manicurist Killer, has a right headlight out on his vehicle! I can't start having him drive around with BOTH headlights working! That wouldn't back up my data! The damn headlight needs to stay out!

<<HIGH PITCH TONE>>

One sec, my phone is going off... Sounds like an Amber Ale—Yup, it's an Amber Alert. It's always so sad when one of these... Oh, it's an older kid?... Age seventeen. Probably a runaway. That's a shame. Hold on... Haley Clark? Why do you look familiar, Haley Clark?... Oh, hell... Wait, wait, wait. Let me check something. I gotta pull up a photo on my computer screen... Holy crap!... HOLY CRAP! I KNEW I recognized her face!

She's one of the dating profiles he likes to whack off to... Remember me saying how when he lingers too long on a bio, I snap a photo? Yeah, well, this young girl, Haley, is one of those gals! But this doesn't make any sense... the dating website is eighteen and over. She shouldn't even... I really don't get this... The Amber Alert picture and the dating site picture... The two definitely match, but the names are different.

Dating profile says Tara, not Haley. The age is wrong too... obviously. Says she's twenty-one... I don't... It's almost like she was trying to catfish...

Ah, fuck. What have I done?

See attached documentation:
Printed copy of referenced chat room discussion
March 02– Server [Redacted]
Case# 608437

PRINTED COPY OF REFERENCED CHAT ROOM DISCUSSION

Case #608437

Date: 3/02
Chat Service: Redacted
M.K. TASK FORCE
Private Chat Room

Lydetector: Anybody else see the alert on the Springfield PD website?!

DoubleDHelix: What alert?

Private-i: NO. Looking now.

GetUoff: Me neither. I've been studying. They update the case?

AlibiBreaker: I did! Came over my phone a few minutes ago!

DoubleDHelix: Over your phone? Are you talking about an Amber alert?

dTECHtive: What's going on?

Lydetector: Hey, can you look up Haley Clark? Age seventeen. Pictures should be blonde with hazel eyes. White girl. See if her family and friends have shared any info?

Lydetector: AB, check with your brother. Find out if he knows anything about this missing girl.

GetUoff: I don't mean to be an asshole, but why does it matter? Do you know her?

Lydetector: Yes and No.

Private-i: All I see is a basic Amber Alert.

Private-i: She a runaway teen? What's the scoop?

dTECHtive: Looks as if her profile is set to private, but I found her parents and older sister. Hold, please.

dTECHtive: Parents claim she's been kidnapped.

dTECHtive: But big sister thinks she's run off with her new internet boyfriend.

AlibiBreaker: Probably some sex predator!

Lydetector: Not some sex predator, OUR sex predator!

Lydetector: Mr. Clean! The Manicurist Killer!!!!

Lydetector: She's one of the girls he was stalking on the dating site!

Private-i: What, now? What was her handle?

DoubleDHelix: A MINOR! That's a colossal mistake!

dTECHtive: Fun Time Girlie... That's her handle. But the name given is Tara, not Haley. Lydia?????

DoubleDHelix: Because cops don't have to wait the obligatory twenty-four hours before searching for her!

DoubleDHelix: This could be the break the police need! If they can catch her in his possession....

Private-i: We need to inform the SPD! It's time to call the tip line!

AlibiBreaker: NO! NO TIP LINE! I'll just tell my brother!

AlibiBreaker: That was the deal! My bro gets the credit and sticks it to Detective Miller!

GetUoff: Whoa! Let's slow down for a second. It's all pure conjecture unless we can PROVE he was with this girl.

GetUoff: Does the vehicle tracker show him at the... Wait, do we know where she was at?

dTECHtive: The family statement says Haley was last seen at a coffee shop on 24th street. Two blocks down from their family hardware store.

GetUoff: Alright, does the tracker show him at any time being there that day? It's still circumstantial, but could play against any type of false alibi!

Lydetector: Here's the thing... The tracker isn't working.

Private-i: He find it again?

Lydetector: Maybe... but it doesn't matter. He's back in the BMW.

DoubleDHelix: When did this happen?!

Lydetector: Four days ago.

GetUoff: Ah, shit.

GetUoff: Bye, bye circumstantial evidence.

DoubleDHelix: FOUR DAYS AGO!!!

DoubleDHelix: When were you gonna tell us?!

Private-i: And to be clear, you never put another tracker on his BMW, correct?

Lydetector: Correct.

AlibiBreaker: Huh? So, like...how have you been keeping tabs of him?

Private-i: She hasn't been, Olive.

Private-i: Unless she's been trailing him? Lydia?

Lydetector: My mom was in the hospital! I can't be in two places at the same time!!!!

DoubleDHelix: I'm sorry about your mom, but you should have SAID SOMETHING!

AlibiBreaker: Yeah! I could have driven down. Stayed with my brother! I would have been happy to chip in!

GetUoff: Order in the court! The site says Haley left with this guy on foot. Any description of the perp?

dTECHtive: Barely. White dude. Tall, wearing a baseball cap and sunglasses. Not much to go on.

GetUoff: And what was he driving?

dTECHtive: Dark colored vehicle, thought to be an older Audi or BMW. No license plate ID listed.

GetUoff: And Mr. Clean's loaner car?

Private-i: Silver, Mercedes Benz.

GetUoff: And nothing about a headlight
being out or any other distinguishing marks?

Private-i: Wouldn't matter. Mr. Clean's BMW
is fixed, remember?

Lydetector: Not anymore.

Lydetector: I bashed out the right headlight
this afternoon.

Private-i: Bravo, Lydia!

25

"Mr. Clean"

Case# 608437
Evidence# 04-291
Typed confession letter- Undated

At no fault of my mechanic. Someone had busted the headlight in.

They'd done it in broad daylight too. Right there, out in the open for everyone to see... Not that anyone saw anything. I sure as hell didn't, but then, I wouldn't have, since I was inside a client's office, my first day back on the job.

I also had parked a block over, my vehicle sandwiched against the sidewalk and bike lane... Customers don't like it when I take up precious parking space, so I typically park in the alleys behind their buildings, or parallel park on the street.

At first, I thought maybe someone had reversed their car into mine, taking out my headlight, but then I noticed the gouges on the driver's side door. It had been Swiss cheesed with what looked like the claw end of a hammer... My stalker had returned, and it was clear, Uncle Gerri had failed me once again.

Unless, there was more than one unhappy camper, and I needed to reference my long-ass list again. Either way, the damage was done, and this time, I wasn't going to bother having the beamer fixed. Couldn't afford to any way... at least, not until Uncle Gerri gave the green light, and he'd been incommunicado as of late. Which was inconvenient because I needed his advice. I was having landlord issues.

I had come home to an inspection card taped to the front of my rental, the twenty-four hour notice specifically stating my presence would not be allowed during the inspection. I found this odd, and even with the vandalized yard dispute, a little insulting.

My radar was up, and for good reason. It wouldn't be the first time I'd been played the fool by a note tacked to my door. With suspicions raised, I decided to contact the landlord myself, who confirmed he would be conducting a property inspection, and it was simply preference, nothing personal, that he chose to do so without distraction.

It still felt off... and if I hadn't been on shaky ground, the front lawn still looking like shit, I would have insisted on being present.

But to be honest, a giant in his own right, my landlord intimidated the crap out of me, and with my funds limited, I couldn't really afford a new place... Plus, I'd boasted pretty big about the body building competition, and since I hadn't even placed, I was hesitant to let my ego take another pounding. Sure he would ask how it had gone, if only to be polite.

So, the next day, as requested, I made myself scarce. Returned a few hours later, my slum landlord nowhere to be found, and discovered he'd moved a bunch of his junk into the basement. Rolls of clear plastic, and a mini chest freezer. Bags of cement and lye left stacked next to a couple of paint speckled ladders. A rusty tool box and wheel barrow... Just a whole bunch of random crap from his painting business.

Which I took issue with since the basement wasn't big to begin with, my bench bar and weights already occupying the majority of the limited space. Overly crowded, the basement was now un-useable for my needs, and I wondered, if possibly, a reduction in rent was warranted.

It would have been nice if Uncle Gerri had picked up the damn phone, done me the courtesy of at least texting me back. But he hadn't, and as much as I would like, I truly can't blame him for what happened next... though I should.

It's time I confess and share what happened to the last victim... "coffee shop girl."

26

Lydia

Case# 608437
Evidence# 05-4334
Recovered voice journal- Transcript- Timeline unknown

Oh, I have so royally fucked up!

Those twenty-something girlies, all too hot to trot for Mr. Clean? The attractive, flirty women, who have been chatting him up? Sending winks, and spicy DM's? They're not real. I've been catfishing Mr. Clean for months and on a stupendous level!

It's been a hell of a lot of work! Costume changes, wig adjustments, colored contact lens... tanning sprays. I took so many kissy-face selfies, I thought my arms would fall off and that my lips would be forever stuck frozen in a duckface pucker! Not to mention the change in locations with creating different photo backdrops, and importune, outdoor glamour shots.

Ahhhh... That's not to say every fake profile was me in disguise. No, I had to shake it up. Intermingle in real people. Their photos stolen from the internet. Which is where I, as I just said, royally fucked up...

Haley being snatched by Mr. Clean is all my fault, and I swear, an honest to God mistake! I hadn't realized I'd accidentally pulled Haley's picture from her older sister's social page. Mistaking the seventeen-year-old Haley for the twenty-one-year-old, Tara! I mean, the two practically look like twins... which makes sense, as they're sisters! It was never my plan to put her and Tara, or for that matter, any of the women in harm's way! You've got to believe me.

The real-life profiles were only meant to be red herrings. To come in hot, raise his blood pressure, likewise his wang, and then ghost him, leaving the perv feeling defeated and hopefully, more receptive towards the profiles who were continuing to flirt with him... which were all ME!

I started this campaign with the very best of intentions! In fact, Andy will back me up! He was a huge help, and really, no one should get mad at me, because it was his idea to bring in real people! Said it would look more legit, and I couldn't argue with his logic, so I didn't.

We tried to validate the fake "me" accounts by having him create social pages to match, posting them on all the popular platforms. That way, if anyone were to do some digging to prove these "women" actually existed in real life, they'd find the fictional personas posting about their interests and hobbies. Sharing their coffee drink of choice, and uploading snapped photos of their adorable fake pets... like any other red-blooded American woman!

And you have to know, I tried to do my due diligence by only stealing people's photos who lived on the other side of the country, or overseas. Not wanting anyone to get hurt, I made sure they were completely out of Mr. Clean's reach, but... when fuck-face changed up his "seeking" preferences, suddenly cutting off ties with all the thirty-plus aged accounts I had carefully crafted... Well, I was forced to scrap each of those previous identities, and make new ones!

I'll be honest. I wasn't as careful as I had been before... I just copied pictures willy nilly from other dating sites, and then went to their actual personal social accounts to pull additional photos, starting anew. Time was a factor! I mean, there are only so many hours in a day, and I was already doing so much... I was burnt out! I had no help! Other than Andy... and even that was limited. And it's not like I didn't TRY to keep these women safe! For shit's sake, that's what I've been trying to do for every woman in my county and may I add, at my own peril! It's so daunting!

Do you realize there were actual real-life women hitting on Mr. Clean? Women who, unbeknownst to them, were putting themselves in very real danger! To think, if I hadn't made it a point to reach out to them and warn them off... or, actually poison the man, so their date would be cancelled... I mean, I think there should be some appreciation for all of my effort!

And the crazy thing? Despite my warnings, the girls who have a soft spot for villainous bad boys, well, they only proceeded to cling to him even harder! In retaliation, and for their own good, I had Andy fake-up a couple of profiles. The hot, good-looking, "He's-So-Misunderstood" type. Thankfully, it worked like a charm, and Andy was able to catfish these foolish women back to safety. Granted, they'll be heart broken when this is all said and done, but let's face it. That was always going to be the outcome with falling for a bad boy.

Believe me, it was never my design for anyone, let alone Haley, to be caught up in this huge web of deceit... In fact, I never dreamed... That's not true, I knew there was a possibility. That there was always the chance. I'm still convinced Mr. Clean stalked Charlene Sutton after their brief interaction on the same dating site. If he did it once, why wouldn't he do it again?... This is my fault, and I feel like my past is repeating.

If I hadn't slept with my sister's husband, then she wouldn't have started an affair with Charlene's husband. In turn, poor Charlene would never have had to join a dating website, thus, never being singled out by a psychopath killer! Same goes for little Miss Haley! If I hadn't accidentally posted her picture, instead of her sister's... not that, that makes it much better, but this poor seventeen-year-old girl wouldn't be in his clutches right now! Lord, I pray she's still alive, and that I can get to her...

It has to be said, there was always an alternative motive to this whole catfishing debacle. Undoubtedly, I had a desire to deprive Mr. Clean of an easy victim, but it wasn't the only reason. The goal has always been to get into his house, and the only way to do so, is by invitation.

Admittedly, in retrospect, I played my hand a bit heavy with Mr. Clean. What with stealing his mail and credit card information, all the vandalization and photo shopping... it would be expected he might be overly suspicious... paranoid.

I quickly realized I needed to undo the damage I'd done. Make him feel safe, empowered, confident... even desired... while at the same time, offering myself up as a viable option for his affections, which I have attempted to do, by making every version of "me" irresistible.

I'm gonna need to segway here, and give credit, where credit is due. Olive's brother has finally succeeded in finding out why Mr. Clean was convicted... Took him long enough. He was charged with bodily harm, misuse of a substance requiring a prescription, and aggravated assault for administering substances without the person's knowledge.

In other words, pulling a Mickey Finn, and for it, only receiving a slap on the hand. Two years of probation and a small restitution fee for emotional damage, despite the fact he pled guilty to spiking a woman's drink, caught in the act by the bartender. It's criminal, but I guess you get what you pay for, when you can afford an expensive attorney.

Regardless, I was able to use this intel to my advantage. Be it a margarita, a martini, or a basic brown bottle of beer, I made sure each fake persona was pictured holding a drink. My intent? To subconsciously lure him in, ensuring his inner demon would be unable to resist the temptation. I also played to his physical desires, making sure I was sexually appealing.

Mr. Clean's type? He's got a thing for natural blondes. So, no need for me to wear a wig, and like most men, he has a preference for big boobs... Nothing a pair of socks can't fix. He also favors a lady with a peach-shaped ass... which I happen to have. The only thing I can't duplicate, is he likes them innocent... but I could lead him down the garden path. Play up to being nervous, wanting my "first time" to be fun, and adventurous... he's been eating it up.

That's why I've been able to secure a first date... which is now a rescue mission. If there is any chance that Haley is alive, she's in his basement, and I'm her only chance out... but I can't do it alone.

I need help, and my task force, they have to step it up. I can't be the willing sacrifice without a rescue plan for myself, and as much as I want to save Haley, there is the bigger picture to look at.

Everyone else agreed, and we've got a plan in place if I find myself in trouble. I won't be alone, which is the most important part... because, in all honesty, I'm sick to my stomach with fear. I was shaking so bad, I could barely smear on my lip gloss.

I even called my parents to say good-bye, just in case. I

think my mom picked up on my anxiousness, asking if I'd like to grab a pizza, and come over, spend some time with them. I twisted the truth a bit, and told her I was going out with a group of searchers to look for Haley Clark... I guess, if things go sour tonight, I don't want my last conversation with my mom to be a lie.

You know, this whole time I've been playing with the devil, finding it a fun game. Always being one step ahead, a shadow within his shadow. But it's not until this moment, that it's registered I'll be stepping into the lion's den, and not only swatting at his whiskers, but sticking my whole head into his gaping maul. A willing offering to undo the damage I've done... It's time to fulfill my promise to Leticia Lopez. I told her I would find out who killed her, or die trying... The only thing is, I lied, because I don't plan on being the one to die.

Well, I've stalled enough. Better log in and let the task force know that our plan is commencing.

Wish me luck.

See attached documentation:
Evidence# 05-4521
Lydia-Cell Phone Transcript
Case# 608437

Hi Honey! Saw on the news they've called off the search for the Amber Alert girl!

7:20 PM

Haley Clark

7:21 PM

Isn't she the one you're out looking for?

7:23 PM

She was found with her computer boyfriend across the Stateline. Shacked up in a Motel 6.

7:24 PM

Alive and well! Thank God!

7:26 PM

R u home yet?

8:25 PM

Call me when you get home. You must be so happy!

8:30 PM

"Mr. Clean"

Case# 608437
Evidence# 04-291
Typed confession letter- Undated

And here is where we come full circle. Back to the beginning. To that fateful coffee date...

I imagine, this is where I should finally admit to killing Lydia Lawson, aka "coffee shop girl"... or "Lisa," as she had introduced herself online and at the cafe. If so, then this letter is going to be a disappointment because Lydia Lawson didn't die at my hand. I am, however, the reason why she's dead. I'll start with that admission, although I know you're longing for a full confession. Hoping I'll bare my soul as dark as it is... Which I will do, but I need something in return. Your forgiveness.

The "Breaking News" banner has been scrolling at the bottom of my television screen for the last hour and I know I'm living on borrowed time. Lydia's body has been discovered. Found buried in the woods, left in a shallow grave, wrapped in a wine-stained wool rug... The very one I threw out.

Soon the police will be here with sirens and flashing lights, and I assume, television cameras as well. If they're successful in their arrest, it'll likely be the first time you've ever seen me... Head ducked, shoulders hunched, face turned away from the cameras with my wrists handcuffed behind my back. It's nothing more than I deserve.

I'm not a serial killer. I'm a serial rapist, and I don't declare that with any pride. It's not a boast. Rather, a weakness of mine that stems all the way back to my college days.

I suppose, I could hide behind the pathetic defense of a "poor, rich kid." Offer up an excuse for my unsavory deeds. Claim that my sick and perverted actions are due to the lack of my parent's love, or my inability to be socially accepted. It'd be all nonsense. I do what I do, because I'm a coward and incapable of accepting rejection without taking offense.

Spiking a woman's drink is a way of circumventing their denial of affection, my avoidance to being spurned, metaphorically left with my dick in my hand. Much easier to slip something into their cocktail or beer, knowing they'll be compliant, accepting of anything I suggest.

I found this methodology quite useful in college. Girls, who hadn't given a second thought to declining my request for a date would, however, accept my offer to be their study partner. Surprised when, the next morning, they woke up confused and half-clothed, their panties gone... Now you know what trophies I keep in my storage unit.

It wasn't until my second year, when caught stealing from the medication's cabinet a handful of sedatives, which could only be used for knocking somebody out, that the accusations of date rape were finally taken seriously.

Here is the fork in the road where Uncle Gerri needs to

share some of the blame. He had the opportunity to stop me by simply letting my ass go to jail. Doing so, might have scared me straight, and most certainly, would have knocked me down a peg. Instead, he chose to send his goons to threaten and bully my accusers, and paid off the college, by donating a new wing.

He's covered my ass every time. Granted, forced to do so, due to my dangled carrot, the little black ledger. But he didn't have to do such a good job, and he most definitely, didn't have to turn a blind-eye... though I know he was disgusted by my conduct and more than pleased when I decided to leave New York. By the way, he's still not answering my calls.

I've been so desperate to speak to him, I even reached out to my aunt. She says he's out of the country, and... no longer under her payroll. You do understand the significance of that statement, don't you? No longer under her payroll means he once was, and I've come to the conclusion, or rather, the realization that Uncle Gerri, under my aunt's direction, was her hired hitman who killed my parents, one of which was, his employer, blackmailer, and at one time, his best friend.

It makes sense the two would join forces, unite in taking out their common enemy, and only too revealing, as to why now Uncle Gerri has clearly abandoned me, the noose tightly cinched about my neck. He's the most likely culprit to have set me up because I didn't kill all those women. No matter what the evidence indicates. I know it looks bad, and I can't explain a lot of it. Especially how my thrown-out rug ended up being Lydia Lawson's tomb, but it's clear to me, I've been set-up as someone's scapegoat, and Uncle Gerri is at the top of my list. The runner up is my landlord.

Think about it. The guy practically blew his top when he came over to look at the vandalized lawn... I've been thinking, what if that burnt message singed into the dandelion infested grass had nothing to do with me? But was meant to be directed towards my landlord? To call him out... "For

Them" might not have been about my rapes, but rather, the serial killer's victims.

If that was indeed the case, it would also explain why he snuck all that junk into my basement without my permission. He was getting rid of the evidence, and making sure it was in my possession, setting me up to take the fall.

There's also a good chance it might be my mechanic.

The news keeps harping about the right headlight of my car being out, and how this fits the physical description of a vehicle spotted by the families of the other victims. The most insistent, being the family of Audrey Rae Collins. The thing is, my headlight was fixed at the time of her abduction.

As for some of the other sightings, in relation to the rest of the M.K. victims, I was driving my mechanic's loaner. Which means, he could have taken my car out at any time, with me being none the wiser. This could also explain why he so kindly arranged for the inside of my car to be detailed... Believe me, I've had my BMW in his shop on several occasions, and he's never offered a free service, let alone a full detail. I don't know... I just find it strange.

But I don't suppose you care about any of this. What you really want to know is what happened to Lydia... Why am I the cause of her demise?

Because I suck at being a decent human. All my efforts to separate myself from temptation, attempting to live life humbly, leaving behind my privileged influence as a Senator's son, has all been for not. An utter failure, resulting in a social experiment disaster, ... The irony? I was trying to be a nice guy, albeit a selfish one.

Lydia, or Lisa, as I had known her, had shown all the signs of first date jitters. As I described in the beginning, she had fiddled with her straw wrapper, had a hard time holding my stare, and her knee was at a constant bounce underneath the table. She was clearly nervous, so when she accepted my invitation back to the house, buying the excuse about grabbing my wallet for sushi, I had high hopes that simply being around Sophie, my dog, would put her at ease.

While she sat herself down on the hardwood floor, Sophie licking at her flushed cheeks and lip-glossed lips, I went about setting the mood by lighting candles, and choosing an appropriate playlist, something smooth and sensual.

I then pulled a bottle of wine from the chiller, and since I knew she was a virgin, decided to help her relax. Slipped a little "something" into her wine glass and swooshed it around, before placing it in her shaking hand.

With a lopsided smile, she'd hesitantly brought it to her lips, and I could tell, was going to try to fake a sip, but Sophie, suddenly jumped up in her lap, and the glass tipped, her mouth opening in surprise, taking a much bigger gulp than she had intended.

While she coughed and sputtered, I pulled Sophie away, then tried to help her clean up. Grabbed a kitchen towel, and purposely brushed a hand against her breast, hoping to cop a feel. The look of utter disgust on her face made it apparent, light petting wouldn't be on the menu.

She then asked if she could use the bathroom, and disappeared behind the door, her cell phone chiming over the sound of running water. A minute later, she came out, declaring she didn't feel good, and wanted to go home, and it's at this juncture in our evening, I could have changed the trajectory by having done one of two things. The result of each, being that Lydia would still be alive. The obvious would be to NOT have spiked her drink in the first place. The second, to have kept her. Choosing instead, to let her sleep it off on my couch. But I did neither.

I let her leave. Suddenly, out of nowhere, I'd developed a conscience, feeling overwhelmed by conviction. Realizing, that if she stayed, I would take advantage of her, just like I had with all the others.

I know there is no reason to believe me, considering my past... and my actual act of drugging her, but truly, I did walk her to the door. Said my goodbye, and then helped her down the steps to the awaiting Uber driver, and yes, I know they're saying she never requested a ride. That I'm lying. That Lydia was actually tied up in my basement, the Uber driver a figment of my imagination, her departure from my rental, a work of fiction. They can speculate as much as they want, it won't change the fact that I watched her get into the backseat of a car, alive and breathing, the vehicle driving away into the night.

The cops didn't even bother trying to deep dive into finding the Uber driver. They were too focused on me. Had tunnel vision, and why? I was an easy target with a criminal record. That's why, after she left, I immediately flushed the roofies down the toilet and deleted my dating profile. My self-acknowledgment that I was far from rehabilitated.

Regardless, it's only semantics I didn't physically kill Lydia with my bare hands. Yet, it was still BY MY HAND, she was drugged and made defenseless, unable to fight off a real-life boogieman. It's deplorable, and I know I don't have the right to ask, but I desire absolution, and I do dare to BEG for your forgiveness, because my intentions were NEVER TO KILL.

If it makes you feel any better, I'm not going to fight anything in court. In fact, I've included a list of names with this letter, women I've wronged... hurt... scarred. I'd like for you to give it to the police and tell them about my storage unit. From there, they'll be able to match up my trophies through DNA to the corresponding names, allowing those women to have their day in court. I'll plead guilty to every one... That is, if I survive what's next.

As I said, I am a coward, so it shouldn't be a surprise, I'm struggling with the concept of being behind bars for the rest of my life, or worse yet, my entire existence being punctuated by the needle of a lethal injection... Though, admittedly, that would be a fitting end.

No, I think God should decide my fate... He's the judge of all.

I've swallowed every pill in my possession, plus all the ones I could find, here, in the old lady's medicine cabinet, creating my own Russian roulette drug cocktail. I fervently hope it will take effect before the cops arrive... Which, should only be a matter of hours, maybe minutes.

If I wake tomorrow, then God has forgiven me, and I will face the music Hell, I'll even take the blame for Lydia's death and all the others... Why should I do so if I am declaring my innocence of these horrific deeds? Because someone should be brought to account, and the Lord knows, I have a huge debit to pay. Then again, If I don't wake up in jail tomorrow, well, I'll be in a prison of a different kind, the flames of hell warming my lost soul... Once again, nothing more than I deserve.

I'm starting to feel sleepy, so I'll bring this to an end.

I wonder if this is the same sensation Lydia struggled to overcome... a sinking into darkness. I'm sure you've imagined far worse of your daughter's last moments, so let me reassure you, the impending loss of consciousness is quite comforting. I hope that gives you some peace, Mr. and Mrs. Lawson and truly, you have my deepest condolences and my sincerest apologies.

Regrettably,

John M Duncan III

John Michael Duncan, III

> See attached documentation:
> Evidence# 04-291
> Recovered Hate list
> Note: The names of the rape victims have
> been redacted
> Case# 608437

LIST OF PEOPLE WHO HATE ME

Retired Detective Miller

Federal Correctional Institution
Oitsville, NY
Inmate No. 7542-1, Cell # 18
Geraldo Nico Bertola

Dear Mr. Bertola,

Or should I call you, Gerri? I'll admit I was surprised to find a letter addressed from the FCI in my mailbox. Even more so, when I realized it was from you, the elusive, "Uncle Gerri." Well, not so slippery as to outrun Interpol Police, or as clever to be caught in a country with extradition rights. You should still have, what? Ten more years on your sentence, nailed for Wire Fraud and Tax evasion.

The prosecutor's office said your fancy lawyer worked a miracle, getting the rest of your charges dropped. Which makes me wonder, how much dirt did you have on the guy? A highfalutin' lawyer like himself, offering his services pro bono? That doesn't happen unless you've got something on him, which could land him in hot water. Sure you don't want to unburden yourself, and seek a little bit of revenge at the same time? I happen to know he pleaded you out at twenty, when they were only asking fifteen. Guess he got the best of you after all.

Well, now that we have the niceties out of the way, I'll dive right into your request. You have assumed correct, Sir. Upon my retirement, I did take copies of a certain case file. Brought it home with me in the hopes of staving off boredom during retirement, and at the same time, having hopes of miraculously solving the cold case, which also, happened to be the only one I never closed. The M.K. Killings.

I am curious though, as to why, after all this time, you've written to inquire about the details. I'm going to assume, it's not because you believe your ward, who I'll refer to as "Mr. Clean", was truly innocent. I don't think you're as all naïve as that. So, my next conclusion is you're dying of boredom.

As it happens, Gerri, so am I.

This will be a first for me. I've never had a jailhouse pen-pal. Might be fun! My wife has passed away and our kids are grown, raising children of their own, who I only see every other holiday. There's not much to look forward to besides the grave, and I don't see the harm in trying to earn brownie points with St. Peter. We'll try to solve this together, because if Mr. Clean's confession letter is remotely true, you're in need of brownie points too. By the way, in our next letter? I'd love to hear your version of events regarding the Hampton Duncan Murders, since Senator Duncan was a friend of yours.

Now, if you've done as I've requested, you've already read the attached transcripts and corresponding evidence. I realize it's only natural you may be tempted to believe the sincerity of the confession letter, but I caution you against it. You and I both know he was a narcissist, and though I'm no psychologist, I can tell you those manipulating bastards lie with a forked tongue and convincingly.

So, let's start by separating truth from fiction, beginning

with my first and only encounter with Lydia Lawson. Alive, that is. She had called into the tip line, claiming she was in possession of key evidence. Proof that the M.K. victims were all stalked by the same vehicle, a dark BMW with a right headlight out.

We invited her down to the station, my partner (God rest his soul) and I both curious. We also planned on having a little one-on-one regarding her conduct. You see, we had received complaints from the victim's families.

It was brought to our attention, the young lady had reached out, introducing herself as a television news producer, using the name of a popular true crime program. The victims, also loyal fans of the show's popular internet forum and podcast, Lydia used this to her advantage, ensuring her offer would be hard to resist. Even so, the families were suspicious, understandably both wary and weary of the media, the non-relenting twenty-four hour coverage, a two-edge sword.

Once convinced their loved one's case would once again be front and center, replacing the latest political scandal or "puff piece" about the death of some has-been movie star, it was no surprise the families finally agreed to speak with her.

I took serious offense to Lydia's tactics, finding them cold-hearted, intrusive, and meddlesome. She falsely promised something she couldn't deliver on, and had done so, to only satisfy her own curiosity. Not to mention, she was interfering with an active murder investigation. I tried to scare her straight. Told her to leave the families alone and stop with the amateur sleuthing. Ourselves, along with the FBI, were already on the case.

And yes, it was true, we had asked the public for their assistance. Hoping to generate activity on the tip line, produce a hot lead out of thin air, but that didn't mean she could go sticking her nose where it didn't belong.

It was clear, she didn't understand the repercussions of her actions. Before she had spoken with the families, none of them, when first interviewed, ever mentioned a vehicle with a burnt-out headlight. But after speaking with Lydia, suddenly, they each seemed to recall its existence, and concerning enough, were unable to agree on which side of the vehicle, left or right, had the headlight out. Without realizing it, Lydia had planted an idea into their heads, and as far as I was concerned, that was witness tampering.

Please don't think Pickard and I didn't take her so-called evidence seriously. We reviewed the tapes. (God only knows how she got a hold of the bus line CCTV without a warrant.) But unfortunately, found most of the video too grainy to make out, the details lost in pixelation. We did agree, by the shape of the headlights, that the vehicle in question was an older BMW. But as for the color? Could have been black. Maybe, dark grey or blue? The license plate, indistinguishable.

Regardless of the quality, we did our due diligence. Compared her "evidence" against the legal, warrant approved videos we had collected, sending both off to FBI headquarters. It should also be noted a BOLO had been issued on the BMW and sent out to all law enforcement agencies, but held back from the media. This is standard procedure, and done out of caution.

As you can guess, she didn't take kindly to my reprimand, so I wasn't surprised when after I sent her away with a flea in her ear, we never heard from Miss Lawson again. It wasn't until almost a year later her name came across my desk. She'd been reported as a missing person, but not tied to the M.K. killings, at least, not at first. Her mother had erroneously told the 9-1-1 dispatcher Lydia had disappeared while searching for a missing teen.

I remembered the case. The runaway, a Haley Clark, had

actually been located the night of Lydia's disappearance. She'd run off with some boy she'd met on the internet, the two lovebirds heading to Georgia, hoping to get hitched. The two teenage kids were returned home, back to their worried parents with their tails between their legs.

Once our department got the call on Lydia's disappearance, we sent a uniformed officer to her apartment building, who found the front door ajar, the place ransacked. The only thing of value missing was a computer from the upstairs spare room and a spendy Nikon camera. It was deemed a robbery gone wrong. That was until Mrs. Lawson, her mother, discovered a USB flash drive in the pocket of a pair of jeans belonging to Lydia. She'd planned on donating them to Goodwill, and if she'd been successful, we never would have gotten Lydia's side of the story.

Her mother finding the flash drive, which held the saved chat room discussions, happened to be perfect timing. We had just tracked down Lydia's Subaru, the vehicle still sitting in the coffee shop parking lot. We questioned the employees of the cafe, and lucked out. It so happened that a barista remembered the odd couple and was able to provide a license plate number, which led us to the door of Mr. Clean, aka John Michael Duncan III.

Imagine my surprise, when I found out he owned a grey French bulldog, it wearing a diamond studded pink collar, the name Sophie engraved on a heart-shaped nametag. I instantly recognized the little lady as having belonged to Leticia Lopez, and with warrant in hand, whisked her off to the vet for confirmation. I'll never forget the joy of giving that pooch back to Leticia's parents. It was the closest thing I could do to giving them their daughter back.

Between the dog, the BMW with the busted headlight, and the newly recovered chat room discussions, I was confident we had our man. Once we added the results of the executed warrant on his rental, locating two rolls of plastic, the same type which had contained Corin Peterson's decapitated corpse. (Not forgetting the several pairs of pliers, an ungodly amount of cleaning agents, and an empty chest freezer.) I became completely convinced. Miss Lydia Lawson was immediately added to the Manicurist's list of victims.

Now, this next bit, I purposely didn't share with the rest of the documentation you've already read, as I will need you to have an open mind. Though you didn't categorically say it in your letter, I read between the lines. You are of the opinion, that though your ward was a serial rapist, you could not fathom, nor believe him capable of murder, at least, not intentionally. I'm about to shatter that belief.

It was roughly a few days after the news crews picked up on Lydia's story, her face broadcasted across the screens of every television within the state line, that we had a couple come forward.

Jogging at night with their dog, they'd stumbled across Lydia's cell phone, it lying on the side of the road, the screen cracked, but still visible. They had assumed it had fallen out of someone's pocket, possibly a fellow jogger or hiker, the area being on the outskirts of town and wooded. The two decided they'd take the cell phone home and post their find on the local lost and found media site.

It didn't take them long to realize the pretty blonde woman on the cracked screen was actually missing, and they quickly turned Miss Lawson's cell phone into the police. That's how we discovered the voice memos, which only made Mr. Clean look all the guiltier in my eyes. Some call it tunnel vision, I call it, "I know more than you."

For example, Lydia Lawson was the Manicurist Killer's last victim. The killings having stopped, suspiciously enough, with the capture of Mr. Clean. I do not believe for one moment, that's coincidental.

Something else I know, that you don't, the FBI profiler suggested, possibly, that Mr. Clean had a partner. Now, this wasn't ever proven, as you know the struggle we had with finding any viable DNA, which is why we never made it public and the case still remains open. But my hope, since advances in genetic DNA testing is always evolving, is that someday one of those swabs we've collected will somehow miraculously lead to an answer and the second killer, if he's still out there, or even exists.

As for Mr. Clean's claims of being "set-up", made the fall guy, a scapegoat for the M.K. Killings, well, I had considered it nothing but a calculated move. His "Confession" letter, assuredly to be brought up in court, would open the door for any clever lawyer to bring doubt upon his guilt, supplying two, seemingly viable solutions. The landlord and the mechanic. If it makes you feel any better, both men were checked out thoroughly. Not model citizens, but each one came out relatively clean in the end, and ultimately, struck from the list of potential suspects. It's my opinion, they were offered up, merely, as red herrings. Nothing more.

I would have said the same for the claim of the Uber driver. We were never able to ascertain this to be true, as the company had no record of a requested ride from Lydia's cell phone, nor Mr. Clean's address recorded as a pick up or drop off location for that evening. He also couldn't provide a license plate number or a description of the driver. It was assumed, his claim of helping her into the backseat of a dark vehicle, was nothing more than a lie.

I realize, I'm wandering off course, but this case isn't exactly a straight line. So, let me segway back to the chat room discussions.

My partner and I tried our damnedest to track down Lydia's fellow armchair detectives, but it's not like the movies where the IT guy punches the keyboard a couple of times, and a list of IP addresses flood across the screen, providing the exact location of the person on the other end. It's much more complicated, especially when warrants are involved, and judges, who feel strongly about people's right to privacy. In the end, we came up with nothing.

What about the traitor amongst our midst, the leak within the Springfield police? I don't think you'll be surprised to hear, nobody on the beat or in the file room ever fessed up to having a sister in communication with Miss Lawson. And for this mystery person supposedly having it out for me? Well, that was an additional conundrum, because it could've been anybody within the force! I'm an asshole and I know it. That's why I always play "the bad cop." Anyway, in the end, that particular lead was turned over to Internal Affairs, where it's still probably sitting on somebody's desk to this day.

I will say this, one of those people in the chat room wasn't playing it straight. The document, supposedly of my interview with Audrey Rae Collin's ex-husband had been falsified. Made up. I did interview the man, but he never said anything about his ex-wife mentioning her house being broken into or followed home by a one-headlight only vehicle. (It should be noted, someone leaked the fake interview statement and the media shared it with Audrey Rae Collin's family, who spoke out openly, accusing our department of a cover-up.)

Now, my theory? Lydia was so disgusted with the lack of information coming from the "informant" that I believe either himself, or his sister, faked the document simply to make her happy, and to get Miss Lawson off their back. Which seemed to work, because according to Lydia's own recordings, she didn't question its legitimacy one bit.

We found the voice recording to be pure gold! Lydia, by her own admission, was doing a hell of a job torturing Mr. Clean. In fact, she'd left a few things out. We discovered after our IT guy did a deep dive into Mr. Clean's computer, that he'd been inundated with spam bot emails, all for enhancement drugs and vacation timeshares. On top of that, there were some poison pen emails regarding Charlene Sutton and his possible involvement with her disappearance/death. The young woman was clearly a threat.

Taking the two timelines into consideration, I was of the opinion Mr. Clean was fully aware of Lydia's identity, (aka, "Lisa" from the dating website), and used the opportunity of the "coffee date" to lure her to his home, the poor girl under the misconception she'd trapped him in her catfishing web, when in reality, it was the reverse. With every fiber of my being, I always believed she never left his house that night.

I was wrong.

Initially, when we reviewed all the voice memos, it was found that the last recording was too muffled and distorted. Useless. I theorized Lydia's phone was either nuzzled in her bra or stuffed in a coat pocket, but since we were never able to retrieve her clothing, I can't swear to it.

I'll be honest, until I received your letter, I hadn't given the final recording a second thought. But you'd asked a particular question, and after pouring over the case notes with a bottle of Jack Daniel's, I decided to call up a buddy of mine who owns a small recording studio. I asked if there was a way he could clear the audio. Maybe see if he could take out the background static and all the miscellaneous shuffling. Well, he said he'd give it a try, and to my surprise, pulled it off.

At the end of this letter, you will be reading the transcribed last moments of Lydia Lawson's life and I believe, find the answer to your own question, "Did he ever describe the Uber vehicle as having a headlight out?"

I hope you write back. Looking forward to hearing your side of things.

Sincerely,

Lawrence Miller
Retired Homicide Detective

P.S. Those FBI profilers are rarely wrong.

See attached documentation:
Evidence# 05-4334
Voice Note Transcript
Condensed to recovered text
Case# 608437

[LYDIA LAWSON]:
HEY... I DON'T FEEL WELL...I'M PRETTY SURE,
HE...HE SLIPPED SOMETHING INTO MY DRINK. I
NEED TO GO TO...THE HOSPITAL. CAN YOU...
YOU DRIVE FASTER? I'M FEELING...DIS-
ORIE...ORIENT...OUT OF IT.

[LYDIA LAWSON]:
WHY...WHY DIDN'T ANYBODY FROM THE CHAT
ROOM TEXT? ... ABOUT HALEY...BEING FOUND? I
COULD HAVE LEFT...BEFORE RISKING...MYSELF.

[LYDIA LAWSON]:
SOMEONE SHOULD HAVE...TEXTED ME. MY
THOUGHTS ...ARE SO MUDDLED. SLOW. CAN'T
YOU GO FASTER? I'M FEELING ILL... WHOSE
CAR IS THIS?... YOURS?... AN AIRPORT RENTAL?
THE HEADLIGHT...IS OUT. OHHHH... OHHHH...
WHY IS THE HEADLIGHT OUT... IF IT'S A
RENTAL? WHY...

[LYDIA LAWSON]:
I'M GONNA... I'M GONNA BE SICK. (CRYING) I
REALLY... REALLY NEED THE WINDOW DOWN...
YOU'VE GOT THE CHILD LOCKS ON. PLEASE,
THE WINDOW... DOWN. I'M GONNA BE...

DISTORTION

**WHIRLING   MOTOR,   (WINDOW
ROLLS   DOWN),   GAGGING/COUGHING,
WIND AND ROAD NOISE**

DISTORTION

**CLATTERING   AND   SHUFFLING;
PASSING TRAFFIC**

DISTORTION

**LOUD   SNIFFING-   BREATHING,
PANTING- RUNNING FOOTSTEPS**

[MALE SUBJECT]:
FIND SOMETHING, BOY? SIT... GOOD BOY,
ZIGGY! WHAT DO WE HAVE HERE?

[FEMALE SUBJECT]:
SOMEBODY'S CELL PHONE?

DISTORTION

[MALE SUBJECT]:
HELLO?... IS SOMEONE ON THE LINE? HELLO?

[FEMALE SUBJECT]:
HERE, LET ME SEE... NO, HON. IT'S RECORDING
A VOICE MEMO. I'LL STOP—

RECORDING ENDED

THE LAST CHAPTER

M.K. TASK FORCE
Private Chat Room

———

dTECHtive: Sorry, I'm late. We all here?

****Lydetector has entered the chat****

Lydetector: This is it! I'm about to walk out the door!

Lydetector: Everyone know their part?

DoubleDHelix: We know! We know! Be safe!!!

Lydetector: Wish me luck!

Private-i: Luck Lydia!

AlibiBreaker: You sure you don't want my bro to tag along? He could be there in a jiffy! Just text!

dTECHtive: All the luck! We've got your back!

GetUoff: Keep your guard up!

Lydetector has left the chat

Private-i has left the chat

dTECHtive has left the chat

DoubleDHelix has left the chat

GetUoff has left the chat

AlibiBreaker has left the chat

(digital code: time response: 3:15 A.M.)

<< Private-i: Profile deleted >>

<< GetUoff: Profile deleted >>

<< DoubleDHelix: Profile deleted >>

<< dTECHtive: Profile deleted >>

(digital code: time response: 4:15 P.M.)

<<< AlibiBreaker: Name change: AlibiBreaker2 >>>

****Entering chat room - Franklin County Crime Watch Group****

****AlibiBreaker2 has entered the chat****

CncrndCitzen: Franklin PD said McKenna was on the side of the road waiting for a tow truck when she went missing.

NosyNelly: Do we know the tow company name? Can we verify how much time between initial contact and when the driver arrived?

McGruff: Franklin PD is being tight-lipped.

McGruff: Won't even release the name of the auto insurance company!

AlibiBreaker2: Hi! New here!

CncrndCitzen: Hello AlibiBreaker2!

McGruff: Welcome AlibiBreaker2!

AlibiBreaker2: Are you all talking about the McKenna Parrish case? I saw something about it over on the Fans of Dateline forum!

MysteryMachine: We are! Trying to piece together the last day timeline from when she went missing.

NosyNelly: Missing two weeks and counting!

MysteryMachine: Had a flat tire, called for a tow, hasn't been seen since. I suspect the tow truck driver.

McGruff: Could have been a "Good Samaritan" that stopped to help and convinced her to come with.

CncrndCitzen: Why would she go with a stranger if she had a tow truck on the way?

MysteryMachine: Might have called for an Uber or a friend to pick her up?

McGruff: Or a family member? Co-worker? Do we know if she was dating anyone?

NosyNelly: All of her social profiles say single. But the newscast last night said the cops were questioning her boyfriend?

CncrndCitzen: Could be an EX? Maybe they just broke up? Or were newly dating, and hadn't made it profile official yet?

NosyNelly: Did you catch the press conference last night? The only thing Detective Anderson would say was either "I'm not able to share at this time." Or "No Comment."

MysteryMachine: Yes! Why even have a press conference?! Waste of time!

NosyNelly: Right? The lack of information being released by FPD has been BEYOND frustrating!

AlibiBreaker2: Well... I might be able to help!

AlibiBreaker2: My sister works at Franklin PD as a clerk!! I could ask her for the inside scoop if you'd like?

AlibiBreaker2: BTW... I'm Oliver.

EPILOGUE

―――

Four Years later...

NBC AFFILIATE: WNGV, SPRINGFIELD-
CHANNEL 23

*BREAKING NEWS BROADCAST
    TRANSCRIPT*

News Anchor: Good afternoon. This is
Andrew Cutting, and we interrupt our
regular scheduled programming to bring
you breaking news regarding the arrest
of what the Federal Bureau of Investigation is calling the most prolific
American serial killer since Samuel
Little.

Approximately two-hours ago,
federal agents raided the home of
Franklin County resident, Ollie

Benjamin Porter, believed to be the "Catfish Killer," who has terrorized the tri- state area for the past five years. Porter, 33, was taken into custody without incident.

According to FBI sources, the "Catfish Killer" used the popular true crime forum, Fans of Dateline, to troll for would-be-victims, upon where he'd create several false online identities. Using these "catfishing" accounts, he isolated his chosen victims by inviting them to join in private conversations via online chat rooms. After weeks of correspondence, the "Catfish Killer", still posing as a false persona, would then arrange meetings with the unsuspecting victims, kidnapping them, their bodies sadly discarded weeks later. Left to be found in isolated areas within Franklin County.

The FBI raid came after a four-month sting operation, which was instigated due to information brought forward by retired Homicide Detective, Lawrence Miller.

You may remember, Miller was the lead detective on the "Manicurist Killer" case here in Springfield, leading to the discovery of the infamous, John Michael Duncan the III, later dubbed by the media as "Mr. Clean".

While reviewing old evidence notes from the Manicurist Cold Case, Miller re-discovered a voice recording, it portraying the last known moments of Lydia Lawson, the final victim of the "Manicurist Killer."

The recording originally too distorted to be of any assistance in the original case, was however, re-evaluated after having the audio enhanced, enabling Detective Miller to discover that the disputed "Uber Driver" which Duncan had claimed to have collected Lydia Lawson from his home the night she went missing, had in fact, picked her up as he stated when originally questioned. It should be noted that Duncan always pled his innocence up until his death, having died in prison after two years of incarceration. He was serving a mandatory life-without parole sentence for his numerous rape convictions.

Validated by IP addresses, it is now believed that Lydia Lawson was catfished by Ollie Benjamin Porter, aka, the suspected "Catfish Killer", and that Porter, posing as a trusted member of Lydia Lawson's private true crime taskforce, had posed as the reported Uber driver, where he picked up Miss. Lawson, her body found wrapped in a soiled rug weeks later.

There was originally some speculation that Mr. Duncan, still thought to be the "Manicurist Killer" might be in partnership with Porter, aka "The Catfish killer," due to the rug that Lydia Lawson was found in, it having come from Duncan's home. After reviewing voice memo evidence from the case, this theory has been dismissed.

With the enhanced audio recording, it is now believed that Ollie Benjamin Porter, the man taken into custody today, was responsible for not only the "Catfish" Killings, but now, the "Manicurist" Killings in Springfield County, along with the neighboring state serial cases, "The Copycat Snatcher," "The Blind Date Killer," and "The Peeping Tom Stalker."

Ollie Benjamin Porter only moved to the tri-state area seven years ago, and authorities are currently investigating all open serial killer cases surrounding his previous residences within other states.

WNGV will be keeping a close eye on this developing story, but for now, we'll return you to our regular scheduled programming. Make sure to tune in to our upcoming five o'clock newscast for any updates. This has been Andrew Cutting for WGNV news, channel 23. See you then.

. . .

Transcript Ended

THE END

ACKNOWLEDGMENTS

Heavenly Father, thank for your abounding love. You have blessed me beyond measure with family, friends, and readers. I am so grateful for your gift of grace in Jesus Christ, your son. Thank you.

A heartfelt thank you to my support team: Kamy Lavin, W.L. Brooks, Sandi Tutolo, Heather Garent, Jill N. Davis, La Rae Collins, Audrey Coulombe, Sandra Harvey, and Heather Payne.

In addition: If I've used your name in my books, KNOW you are loved, admired, and greatly appreciated!

A sincere thank you to my readers (aka, Rockfishers). Please know I appreciate your support, and hope you enjoy this witty, gritty standalone psychological thriller as much as The Rockfish Island series! Your support keeps me going! Your reviews, videos, tags, recommendations, likes, and shares truly mean the world to me!

And, of course,

To my wonderful family and friends:

Your love, encouragement, and support means the world. I can't thank you enough for telling everyone and their dog about my series!

Don't stop... EVER!

BOOK CLUB QUESTIONS

1. Were you surprised by the ending?
2. How did you think it was going to end?
3. How did you find the pacing of this book?
4. What reveal or confession shocked you the most?
5. Was Lydia justified in her assumptions?
6. What did you hope was Mr. Clean's fate?
7. Should Mr. Clean's confession letter be believed?
8. What did you enjoy the most about this thriller?

THANK YOU!

If you enjoyed Safe To Assume, would you be so kind as to put a review on Amazon, Goodreads, and Bookbub? Thank you for your support!

Follow J.C. Fuller on Social Media!

ALSO BY J. C. FULLER

The Rockfish Island Mystery Series

Black Bear Alibi

The Push

False Findings

Within the Pines